The Book
of
Strangers

THE BOOK
OF
STRANGERS

Ian Dallas

State University of New York Press

Published by
State University of New York Press, Albany

©1988 State University of New York

Published by arrangement with Pantheon Books,
a division of Random House, Inc.

Printed in the United States of America

For information, address State University of New York Press,
State University Plaza, Albany, N.Y., 12246

Grateful acknowledgment is extended to The Macmillan
Company and George Allen & Unwin Ltd. for permission to
reprint the verse quotation, on page 145, from *The Koran
Interpreted*, translated by A. J. Arberry. Copyright ©1955
by George Allen & Unwin Ltd.

Library of Congress Cataloging in Publication Data

Dallas, I.N. (Ian Neil), 1948—
    The book of strangers: a novel/Ian Dallas.
        p.   cm.
    ISBN 0-88706-990-8. ISBN 0-88706-991-6 (pbk.)
    I. Title
PR6054.A43B6 1988
823'.914—dc19   88-16114
                                                       CIP

10   9   8   7   6   5   4   3   2   1

This book is humbly dedicated to
my Lord and Master, the Venerable
Shaykh Muhammad ibn al-Habib,
may Allah be pleased with him.

THE END

. . . After a long silence, Si Hamoud placed his hand on my arm and spoke: "There is a story told about the end of the world—how it would be. The vast numbers of the planet's population were sunk in ignorance and violence and frenzy. In one of the great mega-cities, throbbing with directionless, explosive activity, two withered, ancient women, forgotten, dying beggars, crouched in a corner watching the endless, terrible spectacle. One of the women turned to the other and said, 'It is awful. Look at them. Look at us all. I understand nothing. Why? Why this vast creation, this planet, these millions of people in misery? What is the meaning? Did anyone ever know?'

"After a long silence, the other woman placed her hand on her companion's arm and said, 'I remember, when I was a young girl, a long, long time ago, a strange man came to our city, begging. He was in rags like us and he wore a pointed cap. I can still remember the peace in his eyes as he put his hand on my arm and whispered to me, *La ilaha il'Allah.*' "

THE CLERK'S JOURNAL

TODAY I AM LEAVING. I am leaving the Library, my house, my friends, the city where I live. I do not know where I am going. Strangest of all, I am leaving the Library in order to find a book. The only thing I have to guide me in my search is the notebook of the last Librarian. I can scarcely ask him, for he has gone, and his disappearance is precisely what drives me to find out what he found—if indeed there is anything to discover. If he found the book, he certainly has not thought it necessary to bring it back to the Library, but that is not surprising in the light of his strange observations, which, while they incite me to this strange journey of unknown destination, still leave me bewildered. Yet it is from that bewilderment that I have reached my decision. And it is at this moment, confessing to my inner confusion and surrendering to it, that I feel most in sympathy with my predecessor.

In jotting down these brief observations before departure, it occurs to me that this may be but the beginning of a chain of departures from the so-called center of learning out into the wilderness of the world, yet even that holds no comfort for me. At least I want to record the events that led up to this moment, for I still feel that if I could grasp them I would not even have to depart.

It all began, of course, with the disappearance of the Librarian, or, as he is officially called, K.A.S.U.L., Keeper of Archives, State University Library. While he was in office, I met him only once. I worked in Records and so had not even access to cassettes. Once books had been dispensed with and micro-dot recording had taken their place, S.U.L. became the central repository of all recorded information. The Select Committee had gone about its task with admirable thoroughness, blending computerized digest analyses with specialist field supervision, so that no useful book might be passed over. What amazed everybody was just how many books were in fact recorded and made available to the students and those who had recourse to study units. The Cataloguing Section was one of the finest in the world, and my job was highly specialized, so much so that my grade was higher than K.A.S.U.L.'s, although his post was considered to carry a certain academic distinction. His security and psychograph were, of necessity, impeccable, and he was a State servant, not only of repute, but of some consequence in society. His post was considered one of those rare jobs that linked the University to its now vanished tradition, for Kasul, as Keeper of Archives, was solely responsible for the handling of books in their original form and for deciding who might justifiably have the privilege of studying them. Once he had approved a reader's application, his assistants would take the precious manuscript or printed volume from the shelves and place it in the matiascope plugged in directly to the reader's screen. Then the reader would manipulate the controls himself, and the matiascope would turn the pages and also tape the contents as directed.

Even in Records, the statistics of the number of books that had been kept in printed form were not available, but it was generally reckoned to be in the region of several millions, including works printed as late as the end of the twentieth century. Until I took over Kasul's job, I had no idea that his unit was so large or that he had a whole group working under him. His assistants included recorders, who not only kept track of who was perusing what volume, but also of what reading matter was compelling the attention of the free-range students and scholars at any given date, and also bin men, who took the tomes from the shelf to the matiascope and back. The bin men were like the men who stack bullion in banks, usually mutant or deformed in some way, so that it might almost appear that their deformity was a result of their close contact with the objects they handled.

The work of S.U.L. was divided into three units. First, there was Records, where I worked—a complex computer unit which not only cross-indexed all the cassettes, but stored the internal index information of each cassette, so that reference work could be done without the student even needing to refer to the individual work recorded on the cassette. From Central Indexing he could have all the references run off for him onto a special tape, so that the matrix never even left the building. Second, there was the Library, where the cassettes were either picked up by the researcher for private use or where he would screen them in the individual and group booths available for study. Third, there was Books, the central unit of books and manuscripts still in linear script form, which was Kasul's distinguished domain. He was, therefore, the only true librarian in the establishment, now that "Library" was void of books.

The one time I had come in contact with Kasul had left me with a strong impression of the man. A friend of mine who had graduated with me the year before was now doing research work on prescientific cosmologies. His work was considered unproductive by his professors, and non-mathematical theory was officially disapproved of in the State Observatory. As a result, he had had difficulty in pursuing his research into Aztec and Persian records, and a Museum ticket was refused him. He then asked me to use my influence to get him a reader's ticket for Books. His application had already been rejected by S.U.L. when he came to me. I decided to go directly to Kasul, for everyone spoke of him as a considerate and helpful person, admirable both as a scholar and as a man. He answered my telex the same day with a personal phone call asking me to come to his office. It was a bare room, except for a framed drawing behind his desk of a strange circular, Tantric-style maze. Before him was banked the usual communications complex, which he switched off as he rose to greet me. He was a large man, with large hands and a full healthy face lit by shining brown eyes with large black pupils that held you with their gaze. He listened patiently while I put my friend's case. I made it clear that I was not merely using my influence at S.U.L., but that I felt he deserved access to document material. Kasul nodded as I spoke, and when I had finished he opened a drawer and pulled out a card. He punched it through the Records Magnet, wrote my friend's name on it, and handed it to me. I realize now that he said only one sentence to me and that I left thinking what an interesting and intelligent man he was. After he had given me the card, he rose and showed me to the door. As he shook my hand, he said, "Tell your friend that the correct way to study the heavens is with the eyes shut." We both laughed briefly, and the door was closed. I never saw him again.

A month later, I heard that Kasul had disappeared from his post. The first story told of a letter he had left for the University Authority, then later this was officially denied. One thing was certain—he had gone. He hadn't been killed or arrested secretly. He had left of his own choice, turning his back on a much sought-after and comfortable post, a state pension, a house and garden, and an enviable salary, higher than anyone needed for a comfortable life. Where had he gone?

For a few weeks, the University discussed nothing else. He hadn't applied for a travel voucher, so it was almost impossible to see how he could have flown out of the country, or indeed have gotten very far, unless he had gone into the desert. The idea of a Librarian, who had spent his life in the comfortable environment of study, suddenly heading out into the desert region among the nomads was unthinkable. Only two years previously, the International Commission on Nomads had abandoned their proposed integration scheme, and the nations' concerted attempts to settle the nomads were halted. It was obvious, if inexplicable, that they did not want to alter their difficult and lonely existence, and so they were left to their fate by the paternalistic but not disinterested Commission. They were allowed access to certain frontier towns, but never seemed to express any desire to penetrate into the civilized zones, so that official anxiety about their being without papers did not last long. One or two criminals were supposed to have gone into the desert to live with them, but their distaste for outsiders led people to believe that exiles did not survive long among the fiercely exclusive desert clans.

The speed with which Kasul was replaced indicated that the Authority knew he was not coming back. It was only a few days later that I received a telex instructing me to take over as temporary head of Books. (The post was allotted like University Chairs through the Senate, and so they needed a replacement for the rest of the year.) The instructions commended my work at Records and underlined the responsibility I would now bear in exercising my discretion over the availability of the books to the readers. The communiqué was dry and remote, and I felt no elation at my new post. I was to be held at the same salary and I was to be moved into Kasul's house at the end of the week. This to me was the sole consolation in the whole business. I lived in a cantilever block, which, although it commanded a fine view of the campus, depressed me, since I had once read while browsing in Books that prestressed concrete interrupted the body's picking up of some energy source in the cosmos—it was called "prana," I remember—and that this resulted in mental depression and even blackouts. I never was able to follow up this odd information, and none of my friends in electronics had ever heard of such a thing, or of any device which might measure it. Nevertheless, I had always believed that in my twentieth-floor apartment I was daily being robbed of some vital ray and would spend whatever time I could on the terrace, sleeping there in summer.

Kasul's place turned out to be a small garden house, a one-story cube, all windows and steel frames, surrounded by banana trees and mimosa. There was no air-conditioning but it did not seem necessary, as the wind blew through the house leaving it fresh and scented with mimosa pollen.

I took up my new work without excitement. At first, after Records, it was tiring, with the constant necessity of confronting people. The people who were reading the books were not like the students who filed dutifully into Library for their daily Input sessions. They seemed restless and discontented. Once they abandoned Library and its structured programming, they had to handle all the incoming material themselves. With cassettes, everything that went into their heads could also be submitted for structuring to the central storage unit. There the information would be patterned and linked to the intake the student had accumulated since his education began. The computer, having direct contact with the psychograph that recorded the subject's infantile medical and stress history, was able to see where fantasy elements or irrational structure breaks might occur. Thus a man could be steered away from a line of study that would cease to be productive or that might become dangerous for his inner balance, producing either memory block or repeat situation in social behavior.

I now understood why the security clearance at S.U.L. was so strict before readers were given access to Books. Once the reader had that access, there was no longer any control over his intake material, or more seriously, his structuring patterns, which could radically alter with the arrival of new incoming information. The creation of a socially unpredictable unit was hazardous, although it was easy to see how it was also advantageous to the society, if its responses were benign.

After a few days at Books, I began to enjoy myself. Instead of being fatigued by my daily encounters with the researchers, I began to look forward to meeting them, found myself almost becoming involved in their lines of study to the point where I began to neglect my own work on sound impulses in cortical communication.

But just as I began to relish my daily contact with the bizarre mixture of specialists who came into my office every day, I began to be troubled—troubled by something intangible that seemed always at hand insisting on my attention. It was as if I had mislaid a document or forgotten a vital equation. I could not pin down my uneasiness, and while it was not strong enough to merit submitting to a reading, it nonetheless would not let me be. I was on the point of telexing Prescriptions for a one-unit hallucinogen to see if I could free the impulse when it came to me. I was sitting in Kasul's office—I still thought of it as his—when I realized what had been nagging me. I whirled around in my chair and faced it—the strange circular Yantra that was the only piece of decoration in the room. It had been calling to me, signalling for my attention from the moment I had taken over the office, and I had stubbornly or dully refused to pick up its signal. This thought made me freeze in the chair. How could a picture send out a signal? It could indicate, but it could not actively signal. A poetic metaphor, I structured hastily, but my hands were shaking. I sat quite still. I stared at the mandala, my mind racing to describe it in some way that would render it again passive, pleasing geometry and no more. I shut my eyes. "Take it down and read what is written on the other side." I held my breath. Where had the impulse come from? It couldn't be from the inanimate design on the wall—that was absurd. But if it was from me, from where in me and why from me? I got up and locked my office door. The act of locking the door committed me to some kind of secret collusion that was outside the taste of life as I had known it until that moment. I felt like an explorer in the days when the earth lay uncharted, but all I had to do was cross the floor of my office and take down a picture from the wall.

I unhooked the picture and laid it face down on my desk. I abruptly remembered to switch off the telecom, and in so doing, had a flash recall of Kasul's hand going through the same motion as he beckoned me to sit with him. I saw his short-cropped hair, his deep, kind eyes, and I caught the flicker of a smile I had not at the time registered. My hands tore open the back of the frame. I levered the stiff cardboard away from the sides and opened it up. The drawing lay on the glass covered by a piece of backing paper. I lifted it away. There was something written on the back of the drawing. I took it out and held it up to the light. It said: "This knowledge cannot be attained by seeking it, but only those who seek it find it. Bayazid of Bistam."

What followed was a stop, a break in time and even space, as if my body was renewed with every breath I took. And then, calmly and systematically, I put the frame together again and hung it back on the wall, tidied my desk, and switched on the telecom. I did not reflect on the inscription I had found written on the drawing, nor did I give another look at the picture, which seemed to revert to its role as abstract decoration. Instead, something else had emerged in my head, not my brain—I knew that now—but some other center. It had risen in me as water rises in a well after distant rain has fallen. Yearning. But what the desired object was I did not know. It was neither a person nor a thing. It had no form that I could identify, no name that I could name, but without it I was incomplete. It stirred in me, troubling me, wakening me from what had been my life, for this yearning had in it something sharp and sweet that was not of any fruit I had so far tasted. And then it came to me —that what I yearned for Kasul already knew; that where he had gone, I would also go. The journey had begun as I sat immobile in that empty room.

There is no doubt that from that day on, if by any chance the University had asked for a psychograph on me, I would have been instantly removed from my post as acting Keeper of the Archives. I continued my work with a scrupulous attention to detail, so that there would be not the slightest outward indication of the turmoil that was taking place inside me. Drawn by this yearning that had settled on me like a haze, I was unable to sleep. Worse, I was unable to fix my thoughts on what I was doing. Somehow my training helped me to keep up an outward semblance of normality at work, but I could not disguise the broken veins in my eyeballs or the deep lines that formed across my tired face. With nothing to fill the void that I experienced or to still the restlessness that urged me to be up and off to—what, I did not know— my thoughts turned more and more to the vanished Librarian. If only I could contact him . . . But something in me confirmed the irrevocable nature of the official report that recorded him as neither dead nor missing but simply as "File closed." I harbored no comforting dream that he was alive or in hiding. Instead I turned my thoughts to unearthing every trace of him that I could. I wanted to know all about him up until that mysterious day when he had walked out of his house, never to be seen again. What did he do? Where did he go? Who were his friends? What had he said?

After ten days I had found out nothing. Whoever his friends were, they had melted into total anonymity. His name produced no tremor of recognition in anyone except one or two regular readers at Books, who expressed an already fading interest in the mystery of his departure. The complete blank that this senior official of the University had left behind convinced me more and more that if only I could turn the right combination, the door would spring open and I would find out what I wanted to know.

One morning at the office I sat before a pile of cards that had to be reissued. After punching a few, I went into a kind of dream. I was not sleeping, nor was I thinking, yet I was conscious. The contours of the room were clear and in focus. I swivelled my chair around and looked yet again, as had in fact become my wont each morning, at the enigmatic signal on the wall. I don't know how long I sat like that, but as I sat there my mind filled with the presence of Kasul. Yet it was not my mind, for I held no image in my awareness and I constructed no word patterns. Nevertheless, some part of me fixed, coagulated, crystallized on Kasul with such force that if he had materialized in front of me, I would have seen it as an inevitable and unalarming extension of what my inner activity indicated.

The state I was in came to an abrupt end, and I turned swiftly to see standing in front of me the mutated form of a dwarf with an enormous head. It was one of the bin men. He cleared his throat and held out a paper. I took the note from him. I observed that he had six fingers on his hand, but it did not strike me as odd or even interesting. Rather, I noted that there seemed room for the extra finger and that it was not a hindrance to him. He smiled at me.

The paper was inscribed with a clear, open script of a kind one rarely sees nowadays:

> My dear Kasul, I have just returned from Japan, where I met many of our brothers. I am eager to report to you. May I come up? Peace be upon you. Arnou.

Friend of Kasul's

I told the bin man to show the visitor up immediately. My breathing had completely gone, and I had to force it back to normal, for, coupled with my excitement over the arrival of a friend of Kasul's, was the irresistible sense of connection between his arrival and my time spent sitting before the drawing.

By the time the bin man came back with Kasul's visitor, I had composed myself. The man who was ushered into the room looked for all the world like one of the visiting professors at the University. He was foreign, yet the same as us—the stereotype of our society. I don't know why I had expected him to be different, but his ordinariness surprised me. What was unusual about him was his eyes. They shone, luminous yet cloudy, veiled and sleepy, yet alert like a fox's. I thought of Kasul. The man gave only a flicker, it seemed to me, on seeing that it was not Kasul behind the desk. We shook hands, and I motioned him to a seat. I switched off the telecom, and there was a momentary contact between us. Immediately, I explained to him about Kasul's disappearance. His reaction was baffling. He smiled and relaxed back into his seat. For a second, he shut his eyes, as if in relief.

For a moment, I panicked and wondered if this whole business was something quite different from what

I had imagined. Yet what, for that matter, had I imagined? The idea that it was some kind of security situation was a momentary anxiety, and no sooner had I thought it than I dismissed it. I realized that there was no reason why anything should be divulged to me, a total stranger, but because I was aware that there was something to be divulged I wanted somehow to indicate to this man that I was worthy of such a confidence. I decided to take the risk. He might decide I was mad and quietly call Medicine to take me away, but somehow I knew that that was not how it would be. I blurted out as coherently as I could my experiences since coming to work in Kasul's place. He nodded as I spoke, smiling. I was annoyed that nothing in my extraordinary story seemed to surprise him.

When I had finished he said nothing. I found the silence intolerable—a kind of judgment that made me feel unsafe.

"Well?" I demanded, as if it were up to him to solve the whole situation, my condition, my curiosity, my life. After another interminable silence he spoke.

"There's no doubt about it. You were sent."

"Sent?" I thought of the dry telex announcing my appointment.

"You are one of us, brother."

Before I could ask him to what strange brotherhood I belonged, he had risen and was holding out his hand to say goodbye.

I felt cheated and nervous. I had confided in him, expecting a confidence in return. The fact that it was not forthcoming made me uneasy. I had a built-in disapproval of secrecy—there was enough of it in the outer

structure of society without having it in personal encounter. I refused his hand. He lowered his and stood patiently waiting for me to speak. Even his patience
annoyed me, and I felt he was being condescending,
although it was I who had rejected his outstretched hand.

"Tell me. Please. Where is he? Where are the others? Can I meet them?"

"Find out." He smiled his infuriating smile.

"But that's why I am asking you—because I want to
find out."

Quite suddenly, he sat down. I too sat down, thinking that now he was going to tell me everything I wanted
to know.

"I could only give you information—such as I
have."

"But that's what I want!"

"Is it?"

I bit my lip. There was nothing I could say. He was
right.

"Well then . . ."

He tapped his heart several times.

"Find out. It's all in here. Everything . . . out there
. . . is in here. Hmm?"

I nodded. I knew what he was saying, and yet at
the same time it sounded somehow too easy. Like an
equation, I thought, the calculation of which is im-
mense, but whose final statement is a mere handful of
symbols. It was the authority with which he said it,
the certainty he projected as he spoke, that silenced
me. He rose again.

"You will have everything you need. Believe me.
The affair is not in your hands. Hold on to that. Hmm?"

I sat with my head bowed, like a child who has done something wrong, but I felt excited, and my heart was beating loudly in my breast.

"Why do you think I came up here to this office? The heart finds the heart."

He held out his hand a second time, and I took it. I murmured my goodbye. He smiled at me and was gone. My heart was tight and I wanted to weep, but I could not, and a pain began to fill my chest.

Now that the projection of clear certainty had been dispelled with his departure, I began to doubt that there had been any Dr. Arnou in my office. The heart indeed! The function of the heart, I reminded myself, is to pump blood to the head. Yet I could not pretend that this man, with his clear, intelligent identity, could have meant anything so gross as to suggest that the physical organ of the heart somehow contained the cosmos. He must then have been referring to some other heart. But we have only one heart. Or could it be that the heart is not merely phenomenal but subtle in the manner of the brain? I was weak in speculation programming and I gave up, for the more I tried to think it out the more confused I became. The key to what had been said lay in the man who said it.

The pain in my heart was acute, and I put my hand to my breast and began to massage it. I stopped short. The pain—the pain was in my heart, and the pain accorded with the inner state that Arnou's visit had aroused in me.

I had to find out what was going on inside me— never mind about Kasul and curiosity about his friends.

Something was happening, and I had to know what it was.

I turned my chair toward the drawing on the wall. This time I did it deliberately. Already the image of the maze was imprinted upon me, but I sat, eyes wide open, staring at its compelling design. After a moment, I felt constricted by the chair. I got up, pushed my desk aside, and sat down on the floor. Then I got up again and took the print down from the wall. I placed it in front of me and squatted again, crossing my legs. I stared into the vortex of the drawing, my hands resting lightly on my knees. I had no illusion now that the design was going to "do" anything, but I somehow sensed that it could "unlock" certain things inside me. Why and how this should be so I could not imagine, nor was I interested in finding out. I was too eager to get at whatever it was that awaited me. When the buzzer for closing time finally went, I jumped up, almost jubilantly, put back the drawing, and ran down the corridor to the elevator. I walked all the way home. The air was gentle and musky with spices from the market place, and I felt at ease for the first time in weeks. Nothing had come of my session in front of the Yantra, but I now felt confident that things would take their course and that the course would be as clear and structured as the maze that was engraved on what I already understood to be "my heart."

For the first time in days I slept without difficulty. No sooner did my head touch the pillow than I seemed to be asleep. The dream came just before dawn. It happened in that zone of dreams that appears to be suspended in space, wall-less and ceiling-less,

painting - Yantra

and filled with light. We were all robed in white, and there was an unceasing sound of voices in a language I could not understand. I found myself prostrated before a man who was bathed in a luminous energy that penetrated my every pore. I could not look at him, but I felt his gaze upon me and I was both afraid and filled with a sweet sense of protection. He called me by a name I had never heard before and could not remember on waking. I heard his voice as if whispered right inside me:

"Start from where you are. Everything you need is in your own house."

I awakened abruptly. It seemed for a minute that his voice had been not a part of the dream, but had come from somebody in the room. I fumbled for the light and saw that I was alone. Outside, the first silver ray of dawn was spreading in a line along the horizon beyond the garden. It occurred to me that things were not as difficult as I had imagined them to be, that I searched in and out and over and under every statement, thinking first one theory would lead me to a solution and then another. I resolved to take the advice of the dream at face value. I had awakened in a state of elation, and the feeling of gaiety stayed with me. I leapt out of bed and dressed hurriedly. I walked in my garden, watching the birds wheel in the sky, swirling and swooping, filling the air with song. I returned to the house and prepared some breakfast. As I sat sipping my coffee, it occurred to me that the pressure of the last weeks had left me negligent. The place was in disorder, clean from the dusting and sweeping of the cleaning woman, but without that order that comes from living in a place. I decided to rearrange everything—the furniture, the carpets, the paintings. I selected some music, put it on the tape deck, and set about my spring cleaning with a zest that had been lacking in my life for a long time. The simple operation filled me with calm, energy, and good humor. Twice I changed the tape to livelier music. Within an hour, my study was upside down, and I stood in the middle of the chaos and delightedly planned how I would rearrange the room. I wanted space to fit my new clarity of spirit.

There seemed nowhere for the vast foamy sofa that had dominated the study, and I decided to fling it out. The moment I had come to that decision I was happy. I had never liked its cumbersome functional design. It belonged in an office, not in a home. I began to maneuver it to the door, intending to leave it out on the terrace with the garbage cans. If necessary, I would pay the garbage men to take it away, but probably they would be pleased to have it. These were my thoughts as I struggled with the ungainly monster and dragged it almost protesting to the door. I could not imagine how they had ever got it into the house. Halfway out of the door it stuck. I pushed, I shoved. It was impossible to move it. It was upended, and I stood in the doorway trying to push it through. To get a firmer grip on it, I put my hand down the back of the sofa into the webbing and started to move it first one way and then the other through the door.

As I slid my hand further into the back, I felt something at the tips of my fingers. My hand moved until I grasped the object and drew it out. It was a leather-bound notebook of the kind we were issued with at the Library. I knew this was what I had been waiting for and that the dream, the tidying, the finding of the book, all were part of one total unity, in a morning of my life.

· 2 ·

KASUL'S NOTEBOOK

Ten years now I have been Keeper of the Archives. For ten years I have authorized the study of books on every subject. Specialized, abstruse, ancient—every title has passed through my hands and into the hands of men of so-called learning. Scholars. Intellectuals. While they have studied, I have studied. They, their books; I, the process of study itself. I have watched them come into the Library, watched them while they were there, and watched them after they have left. I have seen some in their youth, others in the fullness of life, and some on the edge of death.

I can no longer contain what I know. I must at least set it down, although what I want to say is so total a rejection of the whole basis on which our society is built, is such an absolute refusal of the whole learning structure that determines all our social and subjective goals, that I hesitate even to commit the idea to paper. What I know cannot be reduced to one pole of a dialectic, for implicit in what I see is a rejection of the very methodology that sees things in dialectical terms. I must not even express what is in my mind in this language, or the whole thing will founder in the dead sea of speculation in which my so-called intellectuals aimlessly swim every day of their lives.

I have an idea, and I know that whenever I set it down, as surely as the sun will go down under the horizon this evening, someone will walk into my life and take that thought, that last bit of worked-out clarity from my head and crush it like so much earth until it crumbles like dust in his hands. I am frightened of this as much as I long for it. I've always relied on my head. It's got me where I am, but where is that, that death cannot find me when he wants me?

In the ancient scholastic tradition I hold "Thursdays." It sounds quaint—it is. There is only one entertaining thing, and that is that what began as a straight encounter where the heavy intellectuals could meet and beat their brains out has become the special secret laboratory of the Keeper of the Archives. I watch them scamper like so many white mice inside the cages of their thoughts. I observe them when they behave among the syntax in a predictable way and I note with care when they malfunction, and why. The more evidence I build up, the more I am appalled.

Only my awareness that I am no different from them—but for this dreadful hidden secret—keeps me from announcing to all and sundry that we are the dupes of our smooth-functioning two-unit cortex, the greater part of which lies dormant and inactive.

Clinical study of sundry self-styled intellectuals, who meet at the garden villa of the State University Keeper of the Archives, sometimes called the Librarian. It must be understood that these people are considered the cream of society, and therefore must also be seen beyond their subjective value as being a crystallization of the culture from which they come.

Professor Aller has the Chair of Functional Linguistics at S.U.L. This Chair was founded when the Philosophy Department was disbanded on the recommendation of the new University computer, which informed Senate that since philosophy had been reduced to language analyses it was no longer a fit subject for study by humans, unless, it added in a rare moment of "character potential," the current philosophers could posit a good reason why they should continue to labor at what the electronics could do with such ease and speed. It was not long after that the doctors came up with their new game—functional linguistics. In other words, they applied the last game technique of data-based learning—structuralism—to linguistics.

The relationship between language structure and results deduced from differing sets of given terms. Vocabulary extension and vocabulary change began to be applied to various complex social situations, and the endless "descriptive approach" to reality went on, as did the doctors' salaries.

Professor Aller, then, is a specialist in how we use our thought structures to deal with our experiential reality on a social level, an interpersonal level, a psychosomatic and an unconscious level, and so on. You see how complex we seem to have become. Ah, but I am impatient to write about the good professor. I cannot wait to put down the truth about my doctor of words. He has a stutter. His situationist calls it a signals block and gives him touch games to ease his tongue, and his psychograph reports a communications stress problem and recommends light narcosis.

BEHAVIOR NOTES
ALLER

Lean, over six feet tall. Stoops. Speech impediment, marked under stress. Uncoordinated body movement with a tendency to shortsightedness. Difficulty in negotiating small objects and ordinary environment. Trips on carpet, knocks over cups, spoons, and so on. Particular disorientation at table, with a reversal that could be recognized as infantile. Self-reprimanding when clumsy, has been known playfully to slap his own face to check disorderly actions. Brushes back lock of hair in constant repetitive gesture throughout all social encounters. Always when anyone enters a room, even Library. Tugs left ear lobe when expounding complex linguistic theory. Jumps if touched. Overcourteous in the presence of women. Becomes somewhat foolish in the presence of attractive ones. May even guffaw. Nevertheless, has marked and much observed series of adventures with younger students and secretaries at the Senate. His wife, dominant, charming, disdainful, with her own social orbit that coincides with his only on public occasions, interviews, etc. Eating habits: no sense of the aesthetic. Looks on food as fodder. Uncritical, and will always choose baby food when possible. Likes artificial fruit drinks, ice cream, chocolate. Sugar level high. Psychograph considers it to be above compensatory level and critical. Physical exercise: none. No time spent alone, except in evenings when fatigued. Does information-intake before going to bed. Uses barbiturates only under stress. Does not use tranquilizers. Constant, unchecked hand movement. Neck-muscle pulling becoming more acute. Toe tension constant. Holiday habits: busman's holiday —usually lecturing summer semester on foreign campus.

DR. GAYEN

Psychograph Director, S.U.L. Gayen is responsible for consulting all reports from Psychograph, which recommends treatment and assigns the correct therapist to the patient. Does not believe in his work—either in the meter readings on the subject or in the treatments they may be later subjected to by him. Finds stress illness intolerable and looks to Aller to provide some linguistic escape for the socially unfit. Has a romantic fondness for the insane and regrets the State's persistent use of physical methods of treatment. Admits, however, that with rare exceptions— some artists and certain "visionary" psychotics— the mental traps in which the insane find themselves are intolerably and predictably dull, and this is, in the end, why he puts up with Psychograph. A cyclothymic alcoholic, given to bouts of violence. Police record kept from the press, but well known in academic circles. Small, short-necked, with an emergent paunch. Chubby hands. Spends almost the whole day in a series of futile attempts to cross his hands in the gesture of prayer. Is given, under social stress or while thinking out a position he is trying to state, to pacing in repetitive geometric patterns. When arguing or demonstrating, is given to a high, almost hysterical laugh that can frighten his listener. Aware of its impact, but, to his credit, enjoys this. Married. Five children. No contact beyond permitting his children to climb him when there. Wife has tried to kill herself on two occasions. Holiday habits: foreign cities, meetings with extreme new-thought groups. Has full security dossier and is watched by State agents during international conferences. Eating habits: aesthetic, at times obsessive. Period on macrobiotic diet. Period as vegetarian. Fasts. Appearance: untidy—donnishly and just permissibly so. Given to outbursts of extreme bad language, and

often to create deliberate shock situation. Limits
of his own thinking and mental grasp of existence
have made him weep in public—an all but unique
event in the current historical situation. Passion
for music. Has sometimes brought our Thursday
meetings to a close by playing music and indulg-
ing in strong narcosis when he felt that the language exchange had collapsed. A desperate man.
The only one of the group who frankly admits
what the others tacitly recognize—that nothing
he has learned has taught him how to live in this
world at peace with his inner self, his fellow man,
and his environment.

AXAL

Recognized poet. A latter-day child of Rimbaud,
indicating that, despite the new silhouette of our
society, many of the underlying values remain
unchanged, and Axal was spawned of these poisons. A junkie. Lives in a series of cures that
might suggest his blood flow was drawn by the
moon like the tides, rhythmically craving again
the soothing chemistry of heroin. His only close
human contact a strange Parsifal simpleton of
noble face who seems happy with his company
and rarely speaks. Bursts of energy, poetry readings, cassette recordings, campus tours, and
brushes with State police, then back to his private
world of solitude, Parsifal, and rare visits to
friends. His enormous following must surely
draw some solace from the fact that his suffering
is as unalleviated as their own.

ZILLA

Biologist and writer. Two marriages and two children. Now lives with one of her students in isolation on the edge of the desert, only coming in to S.U. for important biological conferences. Otherwise, tapes her lectures and sends them in to be screened to her classes. Brilliant mind. Original, dazzling, generous. Yet she projects an anguish that sometimes is all but unbearable. In constant conflict with Aller on human values and behavior. In argument can unearth totalitarian attitudes from under any verbal garbage. A champion of freedom, she confesses herself trapped. Has alienated most of the academic community, who are frightened of her fiery dialectics and her ability to see when men project their private anxieties and fantasies onto the screen of history and graft onto social judgment what is no more than an expression of their own repression. Most enchanting of my Thursday companions and the most unhappy. The very mind that makes Zilla so precious to us all is just what makes life unbearable for her.

I have listed four—there are others, and each would make the point. Their "knowledge" cannot teach them how to live in the world. Their learning process is focussed on one fragmented aspect of life, and the culture does not provide them with whatever necessary information or practice would unite their activity in the world with the flow of life around them. This is difficult for people in the present situation to grasp. A truism, they insist. It is due to what they would call the personal history data of the individual. They would say that the psyche structure has not withstood the culture pressures, and so on.

It is clear to me that those who are responsible for the education of the people—and I mean the best of them and not just the worst of them—are themselves utterly ignorant. They teach, but they know nothing. They think, but they do not reflect. They have an unending stream of opinions and ideas; their sentences flow on endlessly, well constructed and clear. They talk and they talk. Their brain activity does not teach them to walk and to sit and to cross a room and to drink a glass of water. Life remains an enigma and a struggle to them, and death an arbitrary end. There is no exception, not one. I have seen them all, and had one among them tasted life, I would have gone to him and sat with him, and partaken of the feast.

LETTER FROM A CHINESE SCIENTIST
(A.D.1270)

My Noble Son,

I write this letter to you at our favorite time of the day, when the first pale stars appear in the darkening sky. I sit now under the pomegranate tree where I have dictated so much of my work to you. The fruit is now ripe, and it hangs above my head, glowing in the last rays of the sun like a whole planetary system. Yet before this fruit is gathered in, I shall be gone. It is important to me that you should understand why I am leaving and also that you should not try to explain to others. This would be futile and only cause you pain.

Do not forget all that I have taught you. It is essential now that you put this training into practice. You will be the last man of this dynasty to have retained the art of reading—retained it, that is, beyond the useless formal act of literacy. So, my beloved and honored son, set down the letter and prepare yourself.

Again, greetings, my firstborn, and receive the salutations of the moving moon as it slants across the page.

You have performed the rites.

You have bathed.

You have donned a new silk robe.

You have saluted your beloved mother and grandparents.

You have retired to your room behind the bamboo screen.

You have lit the lamp.

You have made the ritual prostrations.

You have intoned the Major Incantation upon the Ancestors.

You have noted the hour of the day.

You have seated yourself, adjusting the folds of your robe in a fitting manner.

You have fixed the mind, unwavering, until all the objects visible to you in your range of vision are merged, as it were, like the outlines on a painted screen.

You have observed your breath, flowing in and out until it seems almost to have ceased.

There is now a slight film of coolness over the eyes.

Your tongue is against the roof of your mouth.

You are fixed upon the ideograms of my letter with such attention that you could be reading them as if written across the sky.

Excellent. Let us begin.

In quality of mind it is depth that matters.
One who excels in travelling leaves no wheel tracks.

When you read this, I shall be gone. The wind blows bare the last seeds, and leaves behind dry earth. The ocean bears the seed on its back and carries it to fresh soil. Later, the desert will be recovered. What matters to the wind is that the seed should live.

Here the Empire has collapsed. The soldier is more honored than the scholar, and the scholar relies on his books. The sage shuts his door to visitors and goes back to his garden.

My honorable father told me that his grandfather—long may he be remembered!—wept over the scholars of his day. The yarrow stalks had been replaced by three coins, and the obligatory period of three-hour meditation had been reduced to half an hour before consultation of the Oracle of the I Ching. Yesterday, the learned doctor of physics at the Court lifted a copy of the I

Ching while he was at dinner and opened it at random, declaring the hexagram with enthusiasm. He noted that even thus it was full of wisdom. As he made this observation, a drop of soy sauce fell, unnoticed, on the noble pages of the Oracle. It was always the teaching of our most honored ancestors that recourse to an oracle was in itself a sign of ignorance. Many times we have been reminded that we contain all the sixty-four hexagrams within us, and the webbed calculation that unfolds the reading is arrived at without trouble by a clear mind. Yet if it is to be used with wisdom, it must be understood that the Oracle is the pretext, and the calculation itself is the experience. A lame man may use a stick until he recovers the use of his limb. If he relies on the stick too long, he may become deformed. If, once deformed, he then bows to the stick, he is in a state of ignorance.

I am leaving the Court of the Emperor. It is always through not meddling that the Empire is won.

When the venerable Lao Tzu took his westward journey, be assured, most noble son, that he journeyed as I journey. The wind carried the seed to the west. Now, after a long stillness, the wind is rising, and the seed that is not resistant or tangled in thorn will be inexorably blown across the desert to some unknown western shore. This is the way of the wind. Know that the exalted teacher Lao Tzu made one necessary halt on his journey to the west. He stopped his horse at the gate of the keeper of the pass. Kuan Yin, the humble, the righteous Master, who lived in the pass, low in the valley between the mountains, untouched by the storms that raged over his head, this was the man that Lao Tzu visited. They sat in silence for three days, unmoving, except when Kuan Yin served his guest, as was his habit. On the third day, around dusk, he arose and went out of the room, leaving the younger sage seated alone on the floor.

Lao Tzu, for the first time since his arrival, began to feel that same ease and limpidity seep through his body that so clearly permeated the mind and movements of the keeper of the pass. He changed his position—a thing he would have hesitated to do before, in case it might have indicated a lack of absorption. He began to take in the room and the sunny courtyard beyond. The place was thick with the scent of jasmine and honeysuckle. Delicate black orchids grew along the wide sill of the window. The room itself was bare, except for two round black cushions. The floor was covered with woven reeds. A screen hung on one wall bearing the ideograph "Attention." Kuan Yin returned to his guest holding a wooden spoon. He knelt before Lao Tzu and held the spoon to his mouth as one might do for an invalid or a child. Unquestioning, Lao Tzu supped from the spoon. His whole mouth was filled with golden honey. Rich, smooth, warm honey. It tasted of the mountain heather, but his nostrils were filled with the scent of garden flowers. It was of a sweetness he had never tasted, and yet it was bitter and had the tang of icy mountain water, mineral and strong. It was as if the honey had the gathered strength of opium poppies, for its energy filled his head, and its warmth penetrated down through every center of his body as happens when the acupuncturist opens up a new source of power with his silver needles. The next thing he knew, he was alone again, and try as he might, he could not recapture the instant that the Master had left his presence. Imperceptibly, his mind stopped.

How long he sat there will never be known. Two, three days, it does not matter. He sat, suspended, all body function ceased, neither breath nor heartbeat disturbing the perfect effulgence that suffused him. He was lit from within, as a diamond in the dark, and Kuan Yin watched the glow from his study with serene contentment. Eventually, knowing when the time had come, he went in to Lao Tzu, and the slight breeze from the door made the great teacher sway as a leaf stirs—unresistant, weightless.

That day, Kuan Yin allowed his guest to attend on him. After resting, Lao Tzu set out on his westward journey. At the gate of the house, the two wise men paused at the same moment, each now in perfect harmony with the other. Kuan Yin pulled his right arm from his long sleeve and indicated something against the outer wall of the courtyard. It was a beehive. The bees swarmed at its entrance, and the air around it was heavy with their drone as they went out on their task of gathering pollen for the honey. The two ob-

served the bees in silence for a moment. Kuan
Yin smiled. Lao Tzu caught his breath and
turned to the keeper of the pass. At that moment,
Kuan Yin slid his arm back into his left sleeve.
Lao Tzu composed himself. He bowed to the
Master, indicating his comprehension of the instructions he had received. Once the moment was
accomplished, Kuan Yin bowed low to the new
master, his bow was returned, then Kuan Yin
bowed once more, turned swiftly, and glided
back to his house before the departing guest
could make another gesture of honoring his host.
And so Lao Tzu took the western trail, writing
the Tao te Ching, the fragment of which we still
possess, and eventually taking pupils in fulfill-
ment of his noble Master's instructions.

Tomorrow I shall be on the western highway. I
shall have to cross the great desert, but then I
trust that I shall arrive at my destination—the
observatory at Maragha, built by Hulagu, the
grandson of Genghis Khan, an ironic and consol-
ing fact. When they ask about my departure, let
me appear as an impatient scientist. It will be
easier for them and for you. Tell them that I had
talked of Maragha and of the superb precision
instruments they utilize in the observatory. They
have a mural quadrant with a radius of 430 centi-
meters, solstitial and equinoctial armillary, and
azimuth rings. Do not talk to them of its methods
of work, such as I have divulged to you, nor of
its exalted director, the Master Nasir ad-Din
at-Tusi, who may well be, for me, the Keeper of

the Western Pass. There are scientists and philosophers in that far kingdom that surpass any the earth has ever known, but they are all as children to the teacher who draws me as the straw is compelled by the amber.

Thirty spokes
Share one hub.

Perhaps one day, if it is to be, I shall have a small apiary, but I desire nothing as I wait contentedly for this ink to dry. It is a clear night, and Mars can be seen with the naked eye.
Your father,
    Fao-Mun-Ji

LETTER FROM A DISCIPLE OF THE SHAYKH SIDI ABU'L-HASAN ASH-SHADHILI (CIRCA A.D. 1240)

. . . the learned ones gathered and sat in a circle around my venerable teacher and Master. Now, when I saw this, my heart felt constricted, for I knew that he had not come to Fez to teach, yet what, I wondered, could he expect to be taught? Whatever strange promptings had driven my teacher from Córdoba, I did not see how he could be gratified by finding himself in precisely the same position of admiration and attention that had always made such demands on him and yet had always failed to assuage the turbulence in his heart. I looked at the scholars who sat around

him. Each was the impeccable product of that
fine *medersa*,* each courteous, learned, and patient. The mood of tranquil attention that settled
on the circle was one that any gathering of men
might well envy, and the weight of erudition and
stored information about the sacred science carried by each of these men was truly admirable.
That they looked on my master as the *doctor max-
imus* I had no doubt, yet I felt disturbed that they
did not recognize his state, that they could not
intuit, beneath his poised and gracious manner, a
desperate, almost maddened lover, who knew no
rest and found no ease in any human gathering.

Well aware as the doctors were that my Lord
had come directly from the Shaykh al-Akhbar
himself (may Allah be pleased with him!), they
were eager to learn at first hand the pure
Tawhid† that he was reputed to teach his followers. After several hours of close questioning, I
sensed that the metaphysics of the Shaykh al-
Akhbar disturbed the subtle and brilliant minds
of the Qarawyn Medersa. My Master's constant
weaving between the Blessed Qur'an and the terminology of his teacher's Tawhid embarrassed
the doctors, who would no doubt have been
happy with either one or the other.

At a certain point, one of the learned gentle-
men unfolded his critical observation of the tea-

* *medersa:* a Qur'anic college.

† *Tawhid:* the central doctrine of Islam, asserting the divine
unity. It is not to be confused with pantheism, for it sees Allah as
the One Existent and the oneness of creation as the phenomenal
manifestation of Him—for He is both "The Hidden" and "The
Outwardly Manifest."

cher's doctrines in a judgment on the teacher's morals, imputing to my Master's beloved Shaykh motives that were both shameful and contrary to the Law. His statement was made with cool clarity and with no apparent emotion, although the air became charged with the tension that precedes verbal battle such as I had seen many times at Córdoba, although never in the presence of the Shaykh al-Akhbar. My Master listened immobile to the attack on his teacher. When the man had finished, the silence was vibrant. It seemed interminable. At last, my Master spoke. He lowered his eyes and spoke quietly but clearly, so that everyone under the nearby colonnades of the mosque could hear:

"Our most beloved Master, the Pole of the Universe, Muhammad—may Allah's blessings and peace be upon him!—said, and it is Muslim who relates it: 'When you say of your brother what is true, you have slandered him, and when you say what is not true you have reviled him.' "

He added a blessing of peace and rose and moved with dignity out across the wide courtyard, collecting his slippers from me without a word. After the sunset prayer, he sent for me and ordered me to take his supper and give it to a man he said would be waiting at the north gate of the Qarawyn Mosque. He told me to take the dawn prayer with the other travellers and to come for him one hour after this, packed and ready to travel.

I did as he instructed me, and—praise be to the

Creator of the Universe!—I found a man lying huddled in rags under the great wall of the mosque. When I knelt by him, even before I had uncovered the food, he looked at me and smiled. It was the smile of the Pure Ones and I recognized it.

"Sidi Moulay Abd as-Salam, Sidi Moulay Abd as-Salam . . ." He repeated the name several times and then, invoking the Divine Name, he began to eat. I was drawn by desire to inquire who Moulay Abd as-Salam might be, but thinking it might simply be a name he employed for everybody and that he might be a *majdhub*,* I saluted him and returned to the Medersa.

I slept with difficulty and arose twice in the night. A certain concern for my teacher made me go to the door of his room, and each time the light from his lamp shone at his window. In the morning, I went to him as he had instructed me, only to find him ready for the road, a thick burnoose over his white scholar's robes. I imagined we might be going to Meknes or even to Marrakech, where I had heard there lived a great saint and teacher, but to my astonishment, he told me we were heading for the Jebel.

I must confess I was quite terrified by the news. The tribes of the Jebel are primitive. Indeed, I could only hope that the blessed name of Moulay Idriss—may Allah be pleased with him!

* *majdhub:* Allah's madman; one absent from sensory and reasoning activity, so that he appears mad. Under a Shaykh's guidance, he can emerge as a great teacher, even after years of being dazed in holy wonder.

—had reached their ears and that they were not still pagans. In any event, the mountain roads were all but impassable and beset by bandits, whose reputation had even reached the court-yards of Córdoba. My teacher told me not to be frightened, that we were doing His work and no harm could come to us. He repeated this with an authority that, at least for the time, managed to calm me.

For three days we travelled until we arrived at the beginning of the mountain range. We took the path up into the high hills, and with every step our muleteer looked behind him, as if he had heard the movements of some hidden assailant, but my Master looked always up, straining as if to catch sight of something on the highest horizon. He never ceased from Invocation, in a manner surpassing every spiritual work I had ever had the honor to observe him practice.

We now seemed about halfway to the heights of the mountain range, which rose in terraces each higher and stonier than the one before. The daytimes were dry and scorching, the sun had bronzed us both, and the nights were freezing and wind-torn. As we huddled around our fire with the muleteer, who spoke no Arabic and who, if he had, would scarcely have been able to do more than ask for more money, we were joined by three travellers who were descending the mountain. My Lord called on them and offered them refreshments in the name of our Divine Creator and His Blessed Prophet, prayers and peace be upon him! Apart from fulfilling his duties of hospitality, I observed that my Master was anxious to have news of them and talked with unaccustomed openness. He asked them if there was a Friend of Allah in these mountains and, if they knew of him, where he might be. One of the men said that there was talk of a Wali who lived on the highest peak of the mountains, that he performed miracles and that he fed the poor from stones. He was called—and before he had said the name I had said it—Moulay Abd as-Salam. When the travellers had gone, my Master asked me why I had not mentioned that I knew of such a man. I told him of my meeting with the faqir at the Qarawyn. "Praise belongs to Allah!" exclaimed my venerable teacher, and I saw that he was weeping. He lowered his head and I excused myself from his presence.

Tired though we were, he spent almost the whole night in prayer. After the dawn prayer we set out again to cover as much ground as we could before the sun rose too high in the sky.

We rested only a short while that noon and then once more we were on the trek under a blazing sun. The stones grew flintier, and the shade of the trees diminished, giving way to dry, prickly cactus that caught at the shanks of our mules and made them bleed. We had little water left, but twice my Master descended and washed the steaming animals from his flask—to the confused disapproval of our muleteer. It was about an hour before sunset when my Master halted us with a sign and suddenly pointed away from the path, out across a flattish stretch of tall, well-spaced trees. Neither the muleteer nor I questioned the strange alteration in our course, for now it was the Master who led us, and we both had an awareness that he knew where he was going, though we did not.

The silence was total, except for the continued Invocation of my venerable teacher. Even the buzzing of the insects seemed to have ceased. I paused once to look back on the spectacle of the descending slopes of the Jebel mountains, green and vast on an endless horizon now turning mauve from the astonishing golden bar that was the sky as the sun moved down to the horizon. There was still no indication of a Wali's encampment nor the usual bustle that attended such a blessed phenomenon, but I thought as we climbed of what an amazing man he must be to have been guided by Allah to such a place, for the prospect was so awesome a display of God's creation as to suggest it had been held in grace for a great Friend of the Creator's.

At a certain point, the Master descended from his mule and ordered me to dismount. He indicated to the muleteer that he was to go to the left through the trees and wait for us there. It was as if he had been on the mountain before, and the muleteer seemed surprised. I was beckoned to follow, and we moved forward across the still-sloping ground toward the highest point, which ran like a ridge along the spine of the mountain range.

On our left, there was a bare slab of rock jutting from the surrounding grass. It was shaped like an open box, and as I noticed it I realized that my teacher was half walking, half running toward it. I heard his voice, choking, call out, *"Allahu akhbar"*—"Allah is greater than all else"—as he held out both hands toward the rock. Water poured from the stone, yet when I looked to where the water fell, it seemed to have begun to gush forth at that very instant—but Allah knows best.

After a few minutes, a beggar mounted the hill and came toward the Spring of Mercy, and my Master greeted him. They talked for a moment together, and then I saw, to my astonishment, that my beloved teacher had doffed his fine white robes that indicated he was a scholar and a doctor and was in the process of exchanging them for the tattered rags of the poor man at the spring. Ordering me to shield him with my burnoose, he stepped under the little fountain and performed the major ritual purification in the icy water like any beggar. After he was dressed in the rags he had acquired, he ascended the slope, telling me to follow at a distance. I walked behind him, my heart pounding. What manner of man could make my exalted teacher behave in this extraordinary manner? He was the most honored pupil of the Teacher of the Age and here he was on the slope of a wild mountain of the Maghrib, humbling himself to go before some primitive holy man who sat isolated like an eagle, surveying nothing but an endless horizon of what seemed the whole world, and the rising and the setting sun.

As we approached the flat plane that capped the mountain, I felt the grass soft under my feet. The wind carried to my ears the endless hum of voices intoning some blessed recital. It hung in the dark cold air as if it were some property of the night sky itself. I took one backward look and saw the sun dip below the horizon. It was then, and only then, that I grasped what this holy man had done. He was not looking out on the spectacular green sweep of the Jebel, but at some other sky-line that faced, of course, the dawn. We were almost at the holy place now, and I saw in the fading light that the people were gathered around a tree. At the moment I saw the tree, I saw the further horizon, a sweep of naked rocks such as the Blessed Prophet himself must have surveyed from his cave at Hira. Whoever this man was, he contemplated daily the naked fact of this strange earth whirling among the planets and the further stars. The branches of the tree spread wider than the branches of any tree I had ever seen. It was as if it wanted to shelter all who came to this holy mountain.

I noted where my Master had seated himself, toward the periphery of the group, facing the tree, with his back to the edge of the mountain, which dropped sheer below us. I took up my position near him and strained to catch a glimpse of the Wali, who sat under the tree. There were about a hundred men there and some sixty women. Nearly all of them were in rags. The figure under the tree looked small and was difficult to make out in the dying light. As he moved,

a circle of light lit his face, at the same time making it difficult for me to see his features. Abruptly
the singing stopped, and a man right behind me
gave the Call to Prayer. His voice rang out across
the empty ravine, and I found myself longing for
dawn and the wonder of facing out across the
bare mountains to bow before my Sublime Creator. When the prayer was over, the gathering
recited a litany I had never heard. It was very
powerful, and I observed several of the beggars in
a state of near ecstasy. The Invocation over, a
silence fell on the crowd. Two young disciples of
the saint had placed flaring torches on either side
of the tree, so that I feared it might catch fire. The
saint sat in silence. He surveyed the crowd.
Someone rushed forward and kissed his hand. He
brushed them away impatiently as one might a
child. The silence deepened. I could see him now.
His eyes were half shut, and I thought for a moment he was sleeping, so deep was his absorption.
After a few moments, he sighed deeply—a sigh
such as I have never heard in all my life. And as
he exhaled, we all heard from the depths of his
heart the Supreme and Glorious Name of
Majesty. It seemed to me that not only I but each
person there had been initiated into the most profound secret that man could experience, that by
some bounty we had been led into the courtyard
of knowledge and privileged beyond our wildest
hopes. But why such an honor should be be-
stowed on us we could not imagine, except that
His divine mercy is infinite. The saint lifted his
face and looked now at each one of us—I say each

one, although the crowd was enormous, for in-deed we felt ourselves scrutinized, not merely our faces but our souls, and Allah is witness to what I say.

He leaned forward and whispered something to one of his disciples. The young neophyte moved through the crowd until he came to my Venerable Master. He motioned that he should follow him. My teacher, I was suddenly aware, seemed completely dazed and had to be guided with great care to where the Wali sat. I felt that perhaps I ought to go and explain that this was, in fact, no beggar, but the greatest scholar of the age and that I his pupil was there to prove it, but the whole amazing journey had made me aware that what was happening under this tree on top of the world bore no relation to what went on below in the academies of the world.

The Wali sat my Master in front of him, and the two men sat cross-legged, staring into each other's eyes.

"I have waited a long time for you, my son. Praise belongs to Allah alone."

The Wali stretched out his hand and placed it on the forehead of my teacher.

The last light went out of the sky.

The two blessed slaves of Allah spent the rest of the night alone under the tree, guarded by two faithful followers of the saint. The rest of us went down to the encampment and supped together and sang Invocations and Qur'an.

At dawn, neither the saint, whose name I had learned was Moulay Abd as-Salam ibn Mashish— may Allah pour blessings upon his majestic head!

—nor my Master appeared. They were both in the tiny cave where the blessed saint meditated and kept solitary watch. It was just before noon when my Master emerged. He was altogether changed, yet I could not discover how this was. As I rose to greet him, he motioned me to be seated. He handed me a cup of goat's milk. I was embarrassed that he should wait on me, for such a thing had never happened before. He smiled gently and motioned me to drink it. Saying the Name, I raised it to my lips. The cup vanished, my Master, the mountain, and the sky. Then all were there, hazed as in a mist, and I found myself drowning in an ocean of sweet water. I struggled to hold on—but to what? I could no longer control my thoughts or my senses. Yet my fear left me. I knew that my Master was watching me, guarding me against any intrusion or interruption that might affect the sweet wine that now mounted in me, intoxicating me with its power and beauty. I wept, but no tears fell, love welled in me—for the beggars who only that night I had found so irksome, for the saint who had seemed so remote and had even taken from me my beloved Master. In the depths of my being, I heard again the sigh of the Wali containing the Divine Name. Then the angel came, and of what followed I cannot speak. Only this is permitted. Glorious is the Lord of the Throne. Amen. Amen. Amen.

I read and reread the two documents I had come upon in Archives. There were many things which puzzled me, especially in the letter by the disciple of the Arab master. What happened in the cave of Mashish? Was the experience of the disciple on being reunited with his teacher some kind of spilling over of a state from Mashish transmitted to Shadhili? Who was the beggar outside the mosque? Was he a servant of Mashish? Was it that the Shaykh knew in his heart that *some* beggar would be in need at such a spot and the fact that it was a follower of the saint was then a further indication that he was on the right track? It all became clear in a way that frightened. Each of these letters suggested to me somehow that the zone of experience was not chaotic but ordered, and more particularly that, as our consciousness cleared, we actually participated in the unifying process of actions. If madness was the conviction that there was some total conspiracy to imprison and destroy us, perhaps the wisdom of the sages was that, in fact, this was but the dark shadow of a luminous truth—that the world was a divine conspiracy to liberate us and re-create us.

The two manuscripts translated, I next determined to place them before my Thursday gathering. I was curious to see what effect these ancient documents, which meant so much to me, could possibly have on my colleagues. The evening was a fiasco. Aller was fascinating and infuriating. He quoted psychoanalysts who had swept whole areas of Buddhist teachings into their world-view without in any way submitting to the very practices which gave significance to the doctrines.

Gayen backed him up, and they both insisted that they were sympathetic—to what, I could not clearly make out—but managed to stay trapped in their linguistic maze so that Axal felt uneasy at being their ally. Only Zilla seemed to grasp that I was suggesting that knowledge might be utterly other than what language could contain or even imply. Yet she too was so paralyzed by the anthropological thinking of our epoch that she could only see the experiences hinted at in the letters as "trancelike" or "ecstatic," reducing to an emotional and psychological condition what to me seemed clearly of a different order. The worst part of the evening for me was that they all said that this was the best Thursday I had held and that we should discuss the matter again. That broke my heart. I was the only one of the company who had not been drinking, but when this was endorsed by my other guests, unbidden tears began to flow down my cheeks. They had understood nothing, and I had said nothing I had meant to say, for I could not.

I got up from the sofa, moved to the window, and looked out into the garden while trying to recover my breath. Under the banana tree in the corner I could just discern the outline of what seemed to be a tramp huddled in rags. Alcoholics had recently become a nuisance in my sector, and with a hurried word I went out to chase him back into the street, glad of the opportunity to recover my control and get some fresh air at the same time.

The moon was full in a cloudless sky, and I

could see my way across the garden clearly. When I reached the banana tree, the bundle of rags moved, and from the dark mass of the cloak a face emerged. It was a long face, bronzed by the sun, with piercing black eyes. I realized immediately that he was a nomad. He looked up at me unsmiling.

"Get me a glass of water."

He said it simply, neither commandingly nor as if he were asking a favor. It would have been difficult to refuse so simple a human request. Without a word, I walked back to the kitchen and poured him some water. At the same time, I took a plate of food from the refrigerator and returned to the tree. The man murmured something and silently began to eat. I don't know what it was about him, but I was held by him, or perhaps it was that I preferred his directness to the weary complexity of my friends. I crouched beside him as he ate, scrutinizing him. He continued as if he were completely alone. When he was finished, he belched and muttered something under his breath. He put down the plate and the cup. He stared back, his eyes burning into me, then shook his head, as if he despaired of me in some way. He thrust his face close to mine. It seemed almost black in the silvery light.

"You won't find a camel in the donkey market." He said it with a kind of disdain.

I realized that I, at that moment, assumed he knew all about my search for knowledge and that this was what he referred to, yet the phrase belonged to the insulting kind of naive folk wisdom so despised by my colleagues—and indeed by myself.

"Direct me then—if you know." I could not help sounding hostile.

He stuck his thumb under my eye and brushed at my tears, drying them between his fingers.

"You'll find it." He indicated the vanished tear between his fingers. "This is the way to the camel market."

The bundle of rags rose, towered over me for a moment, then strode out through the gate and was gone. I rushed out after him, but he was nowhere to be seen. If only I had invited him into my house! It was this awful suspicion that had grown up between the academic community and the poor, the wanderers, and the other out-groups of our society. I blamed our sociology as I walked back to the warm comfort of my house. Yes, that was it—communications breakdown between social groups. My thoughts halted as I found myself back among my friends. I looked at them. Aller smiled at me with a tinge of mockery and approval.

"Done your good deed for the night?"

I looked from one to another and tried to pick up from each one of them something of the electricity, the vibrancy of the nomad beggar. There was nothing. They all gave out the low hum of ordinary domestic current.

"The donkey market!" I observed, walked past them into my bedroom, and shut the door.

That night I did not sleep. My thoughts buzzed endlessly around my meeting with the nomad. I went over the whole thing in my mind and tried to grasp what it was that so impressed me about the man. My conviction that he "knew" something was not based on any concrete evidence, and his cryptic observation, while it could not stand the kind of linguistic scrutiny that passed for thinking in academic circles, remained intelligible and authentic to me in an infuriating way. Behind the phrase, behind the remarkable eyes, behind the phenomenon of that beggar was a man of remarkable . . . what? I had never been drawn to the occult, and it was no sense of glorifying the "primitive" that made me long to encounter him once more. On the other hand, my patronizing "anthropological tolerance" of the old culture ("We have something to learn from these people, you know") I had long since abandoned when I had finally capitulated the value structure of my education lock, stock, and barrel.

The next morning I went to the Library with a frayed hangover feeling, raw and fragile. At about four in the afternoon, I left my office and went for a browse in Archives—a favorite pastime of mine when people and work became too much for me. I had taken to rummaging among the Chinese and Arabic sections and selecting texts at random, submitting them to the Translator, and picking them up the same evening from the machine on my way home. As a result of this game, I had come upon several charming pieces of Chinese ornithology and Arabic poetry, a lot of baffling mathematics, and the two letters I have copied into this notebook. I looked up at the

high shelves and the anonymous dark leather
bindings. There was one volume, just out of
reach, that caught my eye. The leather was almost black, but it shone as if it had been most
lovingly cared for. I ran the rail ladder to where
the book was and stepped up to look at it. I bal-
anced the book on the top rung and opened it.
The work was written in a clear, uncluttered
early Arabic script. The style I could not identify, but my eye told me that it was the work of
a fine scribe. I turned over the pages, admiring
the sweeping lines of the characters and the
pleasing geometry of the designs that I presumed
marked each new section of the work. Just as I
was about to return it to its place, a small piece
of paper fluttered from the book and came to rest
under the ladder.

I put the book back and climbed down to col-
lect the fragment of paper. The paper was faded,
like the manuscript, but was written by a different hand. I looked at it with that curiosity one
always has about writing in a language one cannot understand, and then—with one foot already
on the ladder, for my intention was to replace it
—I slipped the paper into my pocket. No sooner
had I done so than I glanced around to see if I had
been observed. Why I should behave in such an
odd fashion, I had no idea. I was "stealing" what
I had every right to take. I went over to the
Translator, opened the tray, and fed it the piece
of paper. I waited, nodded to one of the bin men,
who scuttled silently past, and then took the
translation and the original, stuffing them in my

pocket almost furtively. On the steps of the Library, I pulled out the translation. I read it standing still, the way one does with a love letter, checking that all is well and then keeping it to savor in detail later. The translation read:

The blessed Imam al-Junayd—peace be upon him!—has said: If I knew that under the sky there were a science in this world nobler than that in which seekers of ma'-rifa *contemplate, I would have engaged myself to buy it and would have toiled in the best way to acquire it until I had done so.*

There followed some coding and the word *ma'rifa* repeated in Arabic and in Roman script, indicating that the word was not within the structuring of the Translator. I smiled at this. I pocketed the papers again and ran lightly down the steps of the Library. It was a warm day, and the gardens were heavy with the scent of flowers.

"*Ma'rifa*, indeed." I was talking to myself and saw a group of students look at me and giggle. I waved to them and went into the gardens. One of my favorite places was the aviary. From there, one had a fine view of the city, and I liked to sit looking out on the sweeping panorama, with the afternoon sun filling the sky with color. At sunset, the air would suddenly fill with song, and from the aviary would come a whirr of wings, as the birds fluttered around their cages till the sun went down. It was then that I became aware that I was sharing my bench with someone else. I turned and saw the nomad I had found the night before in my garden. He seemed wrapped in thought, and I was uncertain whether I could disturb him. And in any case, what was there to say to him? I went back to gazing at the golden sky, although I was now acutely conscious of his presence beside me. After a moment, he muttered something into his beard and gave a deep sigh. Then, quite distinctly, I heard him say, *"Ma'rifa."*

I shot around. Slowly his head turned to meet my gaze. I realized that my mouth was open. I shut it hastily.

"Ma'rifa," he repeated. "That was the word, wasn't it?"

Telepathy! My mind raced to reject the strange gift of mystery that he seemed to offer with such ease.

"How do you—" I could not finish the sentence. I broke off and sat, dumb and determined not to be hypnotized, or mind-read, or to give in to any such extrasensory . . . At the word "extrasensory" I seemed to relax a little. It gave my mind the kind of reassurance I needed—that while there was a zone of consciousness we did not understand, there was an unprejudiced and admirable methodology at work on it. The nomad smiled. He shook his head, as if in negation of my thoughts.

"It's not like that," he said, and slowly shut his eyes, as if tired from a long journey.

"I give up."

I meant it. I meant it because, however my thoughts went, they ended in confusion, contradiction, and value judgment, and I was weary of my confusion and glimmeringly aware that I was in no condition to judge anything. He looked at me again with what I felt was a vast affection that enfolded me but then swept on past me, engulfing the aviary of songbirds, and out beyond the city itself.

"Now we can begin," he said.

Moments later, I was plunged into a baffling and entangling encounter with the desert nomad. It was as if everything I said was taken as an attack from a novice, and each thrust was brushed aside almost casually by the master samurai, as if he were waiting for me to discover some new manner of combat. Again and again, he would halt me in my speculation and ask me, "But what do you want?"

I would answer, and his response always made me withdraw my reply. When I in turn tried to question him, he would smile and simply say, "Information. Is that all you want?"

I realized that neither argument nor discussion interested him. Exhausted with my own cleverness and his unyielding detachment, I offered myself as his pupil. This seemed to amuse him enormously, but he rose and stood over me, his expression almost severe.

"It's not like that," he said yet again.

"How should it be?" I asked, still smoldering at the failure of my dialectics.

"Put your head on the ground," was his unexpected reply.

"Before you?" I asked, as if the idea was absurd,

although I realized that I was quite prepared to do so and thought that perhaps this was some desert ritual that marked my acceptance of his authority.

"Certainly not." He seemed to find this distasteful and frowned at the idea.

"There is no God," I said emphatically, and to my astonishment he merely nodded.

"Quite right."

"Then why?"

"Because that is surrender."

He stood over me, and I felt no hostility, no conflict being acted out. I felt calmness and sweetness and a stillness that was more than just the new dark of the night. He was right. I bowed my head and looked at the untidy grass. The lights of the city played across its ragged surface. The birds were silent now, and for a moment I imagined them all perched on the branches in their cages, heads cocked, listening, waiting for the soft sound of my head hitting the earth. Then, for the second time in a week, I began to cry. And again they were tears that came unbidden, tears that contained not a single tremor of the psyche, for they sprang from somewhere in me that was quite unknown to me as I then knew myself. I slid from the park bench onto the grass and crouched in a heap, my hands flat on the grass, one on either side of my head. I remained like that for a while, weeping. And then it came to me that I was crouched, prostrated on the surface of the earth and that above me and beside me and beneath me wheeled a universe of stars. And there, at that moment, with my head damp from the dew, for the first time in my life I felt at home upon this alien planet. Before I could savor the moment, two strong arms pulled me to my feet. The nomad sat me down beside him on the bench. Tears were still coursing down my cheeks, and I wiped them away, waiting for him to speak.

"You are the Keeper of the Archives. But you do not have knowledge. Now you will find it. I will take you—part of the way. There is a book which contains what you are looking for. It is called *The Book of Strangers*. It contains everything you need for this world—and the next."

"*The Book of Strangers*?"

He could see that already I was going to embark on more questions, and he put a finger to his lips.

"Do you wish to find it?"

I nodded.

"Then I shall come to your house tomorrow at dawn. We leave for the desert. You will need no passport. Just a warm cloak for the first few nights' travel. After that, we'll get you different clothes."

"How much money will I need?"

"Don't worry. You will be fed. No harm will come to you."

He placed his hand on my shoulder. It was as if an electric shock ran through my body. He spoke one more word to me:

"Peace."

When I looked around, he was nowhere to be seen.

I leave tonight in search of *The Book of Strangers.*
Does it exist? And is it really that which draws
me out on this strange journey with this even
stranger companion? I do not know. When my
forehead pressed against the grass, I knew then
that I knew nothing. Nothing. My whole life until that moment had been a sleep. There in that
garden, by the aviary, for the first time I had
stirred in my sleep. And it came to me then that
very soon I would awaken. That is why, when
the nomad comes for me tomorrow at dawn, I
shall be waiting.

· 3 ·

THE CLERK'S JOURNAL
CONTINUED

KASUL'S NOTEBOOK was what decided me. Not only because of what he said, but because again and again in his narrative I seemed to catch the tone of my own voice. It was as if he had acted out for me my own dilemma with the formal precision of a dance. *The Book of Strangers* . . . It became part of me whenever I read the name. I could see it, a medium-sized book bound in dark leather, handwritten, and wrapped in a cloth. The same night that I read the notebook I made my decision. I too was going to look for *The Book of Strangers*, or, more honestly, I told myself that I was looking for Kasul, but to find the one, I knew, would be to find the other.

Being in a state of enormous excitement, I did not formulate any plan of action like an explorer or a researcher. I had practically no concrete evidence to go on, except that I knew Kasul was somewhere in the desert.

How would I find him? I knew that the rules of this game would be hidden and altogether mysterious, and from what I had already experienced, let alone learned from Kasul, structured by an invisible geometry. I remembered the words of Dr. Arnou: "The heart finds the heart."

I decided to go directly to Azwan by boat. The desert lay on the other side of the mountains behind the port, and it was the easiest way into the territory without drawing attention to oneself. I applied for a travel voucher and booked myself into a tourist hotel through the University Vacations Department. It was easier to travel there officially, and then melt away once I was in Azwan. As I made my plans, it occurred to me that I might simply be killed by robbers and dumped in the sand, and that my disappearance would cause even less stir than Kasul's. Such anxiety was merely a tremor, for growing in me was something else, something that stemmed directly from the yearning that drove me to depart; it was a certainty that made its presence felt with all the immediacy of a lump that inexplicably appears under the skin. I was certain that I would reach my destination, whatever it was meant to be, and that, as the nomad had said to Kasul, no harm would come to me.

On arrival at Azwan, I went directly to my hotel and changed into cooler clothes. A friend of mine had given me the address of a man he assured me was the best hashish merchant in the city, and I hurried to the Old Quarter clutching his address on a scrap of paper. I found a child who agreed to take me there after I had managed to subdue his enthusiastic imitation of smoking dope. (He danced ahead of me, as if luring me on with the magic word.) We arrived at a small shop on a flight of stairs lined with beggars. I gave the boy too much money, and he scuttled away before I changed my mind.

The place was lit by lamps, although it was daylight outside; the walls were draped with velvet hangings, and the richly decorated carpet on the floor was littered with embroidered cushions. Two men and a woman lay on a divan in a corner speaking a language I could not understand. Nasir, the merchant, greeted me formally, but when I told him I had come from my friend, he immediately came alive. He ordered mint tea and sat me down among the cushions. I could see from his eyes and the slow yet alert way he moved that he was stoned, and I was also conscious that he was observing me.

We talked; I told him of my mission and asked if he had any idea where I might find Kasul and who might be his companions. He did not answer me directly, but instead continued his piercing scrutiny and occasionally lit a pipe, which he would take over to the whispering guests on the divan. The tea arrived. With incredible speed, he prepared a pipe from several small packets under the low table at which he sat, then abruptly held it out to me, smiling for the first time. As I took it, he held the match in the air and said, "Now you will smoke for the very first time. This smoke is the best in the whole world. No imitation." He laughed and put the match to the yellow pile of hashish in the small clay bowl. I drew deeply on it, held it, and sank slowly among the cushions. Even before I exhaled, my ears were singing.

He looked at me with approval. "That is the way." I made to hand the pipe back to him, but he motioned me to finish it.

"Sit up," he ordered me, smiling. "It is not for lying back stoned. No, this is hashish to see by. I will give you another pipe, and then you will understand. I don't give this to everyone." (He indicated the people in the corner.) "This is serious smoke. Wait and see."

I had certainly never experienced anything like it. He gave me three pipes, mixing each one differently and watching me carefully all the time. He drank his tea, turned on some music, and sat again beside me among the cushions. I looked at my watch, and to my astonishment three hours had passed. He ordered more tea. I found that I could not move, even if I had wanted to, and barely had command over my arm to lift the glass to my mouth and drink.

"Now," he said, looking closely at me, "I am going to give you the important one. Do you want it?"

"Why not?" I managed to giggle, but the laughter came from the stomach muscles, for I felt detached, disembodied, a floating head.

He lit the pipe, took a quick puff, and passed it to me. As I drew on it, I was vaguely conscious of his other visitors departing. Nasir sighed deeply.

"I'd like to buy some of this—if—if I may."

He waved his hand as if this was already understood. "You will buy it and you will smoke it and you will give it to your friends, and they will come back the next day saying, 'Give us more of Nasir's hash.' And you will have dreams like you have never known, and when it is all finished"—he put his head close to mine—"you'll find you are all alone!" He laughed and got up to change the tape deck.

It seemed an odd way to sell hashish, but in the state I was in it somehow seemed exactly correct. As Nasir pottered about his Aladdin's cave tidying up, I sat, bodily transfixed, but with my mind racing free. What was I doing here in this frontier town on the edge of the desert? How could I hope to find Kasul, and if I did, what was I going to say to him when I got to him? "Dr. Kasul, I presume!" I laughed and laughed. Nasir glanced over at me, nodded, and laughed back. Every doubt I could formulate came into my head, and every fear became the explanation of my actions. And then, as suddenly as these anxieties had come, they went. One large one took their place and sat beside me, vast and shadowy, staring into me with such conviction that I froze, holding my breath. "What are you doing here?" it asked. "Do you really think you can learn anything here? This is a dream merchant. Is that all you desire, after all? You did not need to come all the way to Azwan to find oblivion."

"Breathe out!" Nasir spoke harshly. He sat beside me. "Drink some tea."

I obeyed.

He looked annoyed. "Do you want that I should say it? Shall I say the word? Always the truth—I do not lie."

His accent seemed no longer quaint and roguish. He spoke with an authority that came from life. I nodded.

"No one else will say this to you. Just once. Then you must decide."

He got up and shut the door, and then came back to me. The shadow had left me, and I sat waiting on his "word," as I had once sat in Kasul's office gazing at the mandala.

"Muslim, Muslim, Muslim." He tapped his heart in a gesture that reminded me of Dr. Arnou's.

I was helpless, high as I had never been high in my life. I could only stare at him and register with what was left of my mind that I was trembling.

How could I exchange one religion for another? What was the point? Christianity had failed, and what I saw of Islam seemed no different. Certainly, the worship was nobly simple and its inner teachings sublime, but what of those subjugated women and what of its long bloody history? What of the sword? Yet none of these arguments that I had already filed in my brain under "Islam" came either to my mind or to my tongue, and before I could attempt to formulate any response, to my amazement Nasir himself swept them aside.

"That is not Islam." And he reeled off a list of my social iniquities. "You do not find Islam lying about in the market place. Muslim . . . Such a man is rare, very rare."

We stared at each other in silence, and then again Nasir began to speak, gently, nodding all the time, crossing and uncrossing his arms over his chest.

"I know where your Kasul has gone. I know who these men are that he is with—yes, I, Nasir, who smoke dope, but who love the God. Yes. Who love the God."

I wanted to argue, to articulate, but the hashish stubbornly refused to allow me to play these games. It suspended me in a reality of immediacy that made the thick roping of the carpet under my hands and the hot sweetness of the tea in my teeth and the light in the eyes of Nasir enough for that moment, and so I simply touched and tasted and saw and listened.

The door opened, and a man stood in the doorway. He was dressed in a long robe, so ragged that it hung about his bony body almost in strips. He wore leather sandals black with age, and on his head was a vast, toppling black turban. The face was cadaverous and the eyes misted. Nasir got up, went to a drawer, and pulled out a note. I registered that it was a considerable sum to give a beggar before it was thrust into the man's hand with a murmured exclamation from Nasir. The man took it and nodded, whispered something, and was gone. He had taken it as if he expected it and as if it was his due. Nasir looked across at me.

"He is one. He is one of the Guardians. There are men in this city that the rich visitors who come to see me look at like they were beggars, but they don't realize that these men are worth fifty, a hundred of them."

He laughed and laughed as though I were incredibly stupid, and as if there was no use saying something that I would, in all probability, treat as some kind of primitive folklore.

"Yes. The time has come. You are Muslim. I would not speak if I was not sure. You will see. Now you will go out and have your dinner. After that you will go to your hotel and order a bottle of water." He laughed again. "Then you will have an amazing time. Then you will fall asleep. In the morning you will come back and see me."

I wanted to say that I could not get up, let alone face the jostling city and the prospect of dining alone. What in fact happened was that I got up, said my farewells, and did exactly as he had instructed.

For three days, I kept to the same routine. In the morning, I set out from the hotel; in the evening, I set out for supper. I had bought a considerable weight from Nasir, thinking that would keep me comfortably supplied and assured that with such pure and remarkable "white hash" I could not fail to tune in to the movements of my quarry. But that was not how it was to be. On the fourth day, I awoke and went to prepare my morning pipe. I unwrapped the pale golden "white" hashish and stared at it. I held the pipe in my hands, but did not fill it. I put it down. I covered the hashish, wrapped it in a large envelope, and set out for Nasir's, strangely elated and eager to see him.

I handed him the package and told him I did not want it, nor did I want any money back. I had stopped smoking. He looked at me for a moment and then he frowned.

"You have given it up?"

"No. It gave me up."

His face filled with delight. "Ah! It is the God has taken it away from you. That is something else. That is very important." He put away the hashish and came back with a set of small ivory beads threaded with one long piece at the end. He gave them to me after holding them over the burning censer that fumed incense.

"You will find what you are seeking."

Before I said my farewell, I was laden with gifts

far in excess of the amount that had been returned to him.

A week later I had become a Muslim, and, turbanned and robed, I continued on my journey.

I headed inland for the ancient university town of Nahb. It occurred to me that the place, being rich in spiritual tradition, might conceivably still be the haunt of the men of the learning sought by Kasul. I took lodgings, this time in a small hotel within the walls of the old city. My days were spent learning the language and accustoming myself to the ritual prostrations and to listening to the Qur'an being recited in the little mosque beside my hotel. It was several weeks before it came to me that I had lost sight of my original goal. I was so overwhelmed with the fact that I had everything to learn that I had no time to think of Kasul and no restlessness to spur me on my way. The troubled yearning in my heart seemed to have been stilled. Perhaps it was the prayer time that brought this calm to me, but I now felt a sweetness and a stillness inside me that were completely new to my life. Only when I recalled my initial reason for setting out did the old turbulence rise in me, and I rushed out of my hotel and walked in the market, chaotically going over the possibilities of how I might contact Kasul.

Discontent grew in me as I walked. I climbed the hill outside the city wall and looked down on the setting sun and the lights being lit on the minarets to signal the sunset prayer. From the three hundred and sixty-five mosques came the Ezan, voice folding into voice in an intricate vibrating pattern of otherworldly force. I was filled with sadness and felt the soft edge of self-pity as I contemplated my lot. What had I done? Had I merely exchanged one religion for another? Certainly the new one was preferable in its utter simplicity, in its theology and its rites, but I had experienced nothing outside the realm of thought and feeling; I had entered no mystical temple of knowledge. I had no Master, I belonged to no brotherhood of wisdom. I remained, without doubt, the same troubled soul I had been at the Library.

As I climbed down the steep steps back into the city, a man younger than myself, with a flowing white robe that billowed as he moved, came toward me. Although he was climbing the steps, he gave no indication of effort and seemed to float upward. He was bareheaded, and his black curling hair was cut close to his head. He held something in his right hand—held it out almost as if he were offering it to some invisible companion. He was beautiful, and vibrations of some enraptured joy came from him in waves. He was oblivious to me as he came up the hill, just as he was unaware of the steps he climbed, yet unerringly he ascended, his glowing eyes staring up ahead.

The first thought that flashed into my mind was that he was stoned. The vibrations, the slight tremor of absence at the center of his being suggested it. But as he approached I changed my mind, deciding that he was not high, but mad. The word "catatonic" came to me as I caught the glazed, empty face, but as he passed me and the radiant energy flowed over me with all the immediacy of rain, I knew that he was not mad. I saw what he held in his hands and I heard his deep, urgent voice.

He held a necklace of wooden beads. He moved them through his hand, flicking the index finger, and with each bead he exclaimed, "Allah. Allah. Allah. Allah. Allah . . ." All my calm was disrupted, the twilight luxury of self-pity vanished, and again there surged in me the turbulent energy that had driven me from my job, my friends, my home. It was as if a great ship had sailed close to my small craft, and I had been tossed in its wake, lifted and tilted precariously on the wave made by its passing. I hurried to the mosque and performed the ritual washing, splashing the icy water on my face as if trying to recover a lost sanity.

The ritual prostrations over, I sat cross-legged, my back leaning against one of the mosque pillars facing the *mihrab.* * As I looked through the long colonnade, I tried to settle my heart's turbulence, but I had no control over my thoughts. They ran riot through my head like an army laying waste to a city. I felt as if the man on the steps had lanced me and now the poisons flowed from the open wound.

"*As-salaam al alaikum.*"

It was repeated before I realized I was being addressed.

"And upon you, peace," I replied. "And the mercy of Allah."

An old man in a long coiled turban and a beard cropped to within a few days' growth was looking at me with a gentle smile. His eyes were dim, as if he were half

---

* *mihrab:* the prayer niche indicating the direction of the Ka'aba in Mecca.

blind or had wept much, and his smile was detached, as if he smiled at something in a dream.

"You are distracted, hmm? But when you pray"—he wagged his finger negatively—"Allah!" He pointed upward with his index finger. "I could see what sort of man you were as you prayed. That is not right. When you pray—every move, every word, just . . . so. *Allahu akhbar.*"

He declared the Divine Name with awe, letting the second syllable vibrate into silence before finishing the Takbir, and then, bringing his two hands from behind his ears, fingers splayed open and loose, he let them drop onto his lap.

"You must be anonymous. Invisible. Be the *salat.* * Turn away from yourself."

Impulsively and gratefully, I grasped his hand. He patted me on the arm like a child. After a while, I told him about the mad boy I had seen on the hill. He nodded as I spoke and shut his eyes. *"Majdhub.* Not mad, for he is not lost. He is"—he laughed—"drunk. Drunk with love. Bathed in wine. Crystallized in honey. *Majdhub.*" He repeated the word with a certain satisfaction and gaiety that intrigued me. "What a little thing our love is! Can we even call it love? Not very far—hmm?—we will embark on the ocean. Aren't you afraid? No? Ah! but you must be."

He rose and blessed me and said farewell. He walked down the long avenue of arches and out across the mosaic courtyard to the great door of the mosque.

* *salat:* the five obligatory prostrations the Muslim must make every day.

I had not asked him any of the questions I had meant to when he started to talk to me, but the moment had not seemed right. I smiled contentedly, for somehow I knew we would meet again. In the meantime, there was the prayer to be said again, the utterly complete ritual of self-obliteration, the power of which I had just been given the first inkling. I moved nearer to the *mihrab,* silently made the Niyat, or Intention, raised my hands to behind my ears, and declaring the Takbir, tried to capture some of the awe and splendor of the Divine Name that the old man had indicated to me.

After the prayer, I again took up my position against the pillar and reflected on my situation. As I thought about Kasul, it occurred to me that he had been but a form, a pointer to something else that I sought, just as Nasir's pronouncement of the word "Muslim" had not changed my direction, but merely confirmed something that had already happened. As the rites became familiar to me, I thirsted for more knowledge, and I saw that the rites were a form of courtesy that could grow into an affection that, in time, might become love. What I needed was good company—quite simply to be with people whose lives were set in the same direction as my own and who could help me taste and experience anew. I thought again of the *majdhub,* the holy madman who was not mad at all, but immersed in the very ocean whose shore I sought. Suddenly it came to me that he was part of a spiritual structure and that if he existed, then the whole thing existed, that if there were *majdhub,* then there were masters and that, in this dark age, the saints were still with us. The word had been so devalued by the Christians, with their appointment by committee and their political canonizations, that it was difficult to recapture the idea of "sainthood" as being a station of spiritual knowledge and gnosis. In Islam, the word did not exist, the closest approximation being "Auliya," the "Friends of Allah," indicating the sublime intimacy of their inner state with Allah. I had started to read of the Friends of Allah and had been profoundly moved by the lives of the Imam of the Shaykhs al-Junayd of Bagdad and his disciple Shibli, of Bayazid of Bistam, whose coded paradox had first stirred my heart so many months ago. Now I was filled with the excitement of this new possibility that seemed more and more certain as I pondered it—a living Shaykh of Instruction. I had to find him.

My experience so far had shown me that these desires were not fulfilled until I surrendered them. The more I struggled, the more distant a hope became. I no longer sought to discipline myself or struggle after or desire. I knew I had to relearn the nature of my life. There surged in me this new thirst for a spiritual master, but what would this new desire do to me? Certainly it was preferable to an evil desire—or was it, in fact, the same? My new desire could only unsettle me and drive me out again into the streets and onto the sands of the desert at the mercy of the winds and the nomads. How could I begin to find such a man? No, I would do nothing. I recalled Dr. Arnou and our meeting in my office. I would not ask, I would not look, I would not keep my ears open. I would go on as I had been doing. I would study and learn and keep company with the kind old man who had guided me that day. It would be hard, but I was determined to try. I rose, walked across the courtyard and out into the street, and headed for my hotel.

When I got back, there was a note for me. A friend on vacation had seen me in the souks and had found out where I was staying. He hoped we could dine together that evening. On the one hand, I was worried that the rhythm of a man on holiday and the rather intense pattern of my own activity might clash disastrously, but on the other, I found myself eager for the comfort of a contact with the old life. It was not that I had the slightest wish to return home, but nonetheless it would be good to have some news. I smiled to myself at the idea that I was becoming just like a conventional traveller, for even in my gloomiest moments I knew it was not like that.

My visitor was a lecturer in communications at the State University. We met in the café opposite my hotel. I was pleased to see him, but noticed that he was rather guarded in his greeting and reflected that this was odd, since it was he who had sought me out. We ordered mint tea and exchanged the usual pleasantries about travel and our hotels. The tea arrived. As he poured it, he addressed me nervously, almost under his breath: "I think I ought to tell you. I've—I've—become a Muslim."

I began to laugh, and he knew immediately that I was not laughing at him. After a succession of pots of steaming tea, he had agreed to come with me on the next stage of my journey, should such a stage materialize. Somehow our meeting confirmed to me that it had indeed just begun.

Our next days were spent together. We visited the souks, attended the mosque, and drove in his car around the hills that sheltered the ancient city. We visited the sanctuary of a great Wali, who lay buried in a small medieval village on the side of a bare mountain. The place baked in the hot sun, and we almost passed out from the heat as we walked through the stuffy narrow lanes to the sanctuary. The moment we entered the mosque, however, all was the cool, clear stillness we had come to expect from places of prayer. Yet I was not prepared for the atmosphere in the high domed hall where the great saint lay in his carved stone resting place. It was as if we had entered a swimming pool. The air seemed to envelop us. It had density and texture like water and energy like an electromagnetic field. I saw some devotees approach the tomb, and raising the velvet covering, kiss the grill and peer into the dark toward the silent center of our concentration. I did the same. My nostrils tingled with the clean smoke of sandalwood as I whispered my message to the saint. I asked the blessing of Allah upon him and thanked Him for the gift of His Perfect Ones to us. Then I asked the Wali to ask the Prophet—blessings and peace be upon him!—to ask the Lord to guide me to His Shaykh. When we left the sanctuary, neither of us could speak, and we drove back to Nahb in silence.

The next morning found my travelling companion with a slight fever, and he wanted to spend the day resting. Full of energy, I decided to go out and buy some presents to send to the friends I found myself unable to write to, so I telephoned a student who had served as guide in my first days here. By mid-afternoon, we were both laden with small parcels and headed back to the hotel.

I saw the dervish from a long was off, and the second he came into view I began to sense waves emanating from my solar plexus and extending to the tips of my fingers. He was an old man, but powerful in a wiry, bony way. Crinkly grey hair cascaded down onto his shoulders from under a faded pointed red felt hat. His pants were the baggy kind that laced under the knees, and his shirt was gathered loosely at the waist like a dancer's. He leaned heavily upon a wooden staff that was capped with a large piece of carved amber. Around his neck, too, was amber, strung in balls the size of a knuckle. Whoever he was, I knew he was no ordinary beggar. He was like a beacon of light moving through the dark souks. I felt his radiance, though I was unable to see it. With every step nearer that he took, the intensity of his presence increased. I could not move and stood stock-still as he thumped past me, digging his staff into the cracks between the cobbles. He seemed oblivious of me and the market and the teeming crowds.

"He is a very holy man," whispered the student, as if pointing out some architectural detail of importance. I nodded and tried to say something, but was so agitated that I couldn't think clearly. The student was aware that, for some reason, I desired to talk with the man and hastened to explain that it was not possible. Such men, he said, were very holy and you could not address them unless they came to you. I pleaded with him, and as we spoke I dragged the boy along behind the holy man, afraid that I might lose him in the crowded market. I urged him to explain that I was a foreigner who had just embraced Islam. That, I felt, might make him speak a few

words, pressing though I was upon the Sunna by asking
for attention. Respectfully, the student moved in front of
the old man and bowed as he greeted him. I watched
as the two of them, a few paces away, abruptly entered into converse. The man turned and stared, or
rather glared, at me. He gave out something that I
had not experienced up until then, something ferocious, and yet, despite or because of this ferocity, he
was bathed in spirituality. His eyes burned into me
for a few seconds, and then he turned and said a few
words in Arabic. A moment later, he was hurrying on
his way. I grasped eagerly at the translation: "Tell
him he has done right. Congratulate him. Tell him he
must have courage. Tell him to go on."

All sense of courtesy left me. The meeting had happened, had been meant to happen. I wanted more. I
urged the poor boy to run after him again. I wanted to
speak with the holy man. Surely he had some message of
great import for me. Dutifully, the student caught up
with him again. We now stood a frozen triangle in the
moving sea of people leaving the market place for home.
He said one sentence in a clear voice and turned and
disappeared into the crowd.

"What did he say? What was it?"

The boy seemed stunned. He looked out into the
streaming crowd of backs to where, a moment ago, the
holy man had stood, and then he looked at me, and I saw
that he too sensed the man's inner majesty.

"He said, 'I have nothing to say—to anybody.'"

I piled the parcels into the student's arms and sent
him back to the hotel. I wanted to be alone and I wanted
to pray. The effect of this extraordinary man had thrown

me into an even greater turmoil than my meeting with
the *majdhub*. I went to the Great Mosque and performed
the ritual washing in the marble fountain and then
crossed the wide courtyard into the cool shade of the
colonnades. I sat in a quiet corner after making the two
prostrations customary on entering a mosque. I realized
that it was impossible for me to grasp the inner state of
consciousness that led a man to make the astonishing
remark with which he had left us. I could imagine it, I
could appreciate it, but I could not possibly know it
directly. His condition made me aware for the first time
of the length of the journey, and then it came to me that
if I was far from such lofty detachment from the world
of men, the dervish himself was far from the sublime and
radiant peace of the most holy and perfect saints. Somehow, the encounter with the felt-capped beggar had
brought me awake. I felt for the first time acutely aware
of a whole network of spiritual energies, of a web of
lovers moving through the ancient city, outwardly invisible but inwardly connected. It was as if the ancient
city, lying there among the hills, bustled with mercan-
tile activity, love affairs and deaths, and the myriad
distractions and drives that urge men on through their
lives, but that when you looked again at these same
busy narrow streets and high-walled houses so full of
ambitions and desires, they all became transformed.
Just as a man's outward appearance can veil his inner
condition, so with the city. I saw it as a honeycomb,
geometric, orderly, everything in its place. The apparently chaotic swarming of the bees was nothing less
than the planned filling of the comb. All that buzzing
and flying and stinging was in order that the honey

should be made ready. This was the purpose of the hive.

On my way out of the mosque, I was approached by a smiling, round-faced man, elegantly dressed in a white robe and carrying his finely tooled yellow slippers in his left hand. He welcomed me and said how happy he was to see a Muslim from another country visiting his city. We talked for a moment together, and I enjoyed the ease of this simple exchange after the adventure of the afternoon, yet even as we talked it seemed that my adventure was not over, for across the courtyard I saw the dervish come into the mosque and head for the fountains. At that moment, the friendly stranger said to me, "Have you any knowledge of Tasawwuf?"* At any other time, I suppose I would have rejoiced in this conversation, but faced with the presence of the beggar, whose power I could feel even at a distance, I could only point to him and say, "There is Tasawwuf—walking."

The man smiled a little superciliously and said, "My good friend, you are a foreigner and you mustn't be misled by the exotic. You see a man bizarrely dressed and then imagine all kinds of things."

Across the courtyard the beggar stood ready to perform his ritual washing. He looked over at us and flung his amber-handled staff to the ground. He lifted the giant amber beads from around his neck and put these too on the ground. He held out his arms by his sides and stood before us barefoot in his simple cotton shirt and pants. We both stared at him, and then I looked at the man beside me and observed that, in his

Tasawwuf: Sufism.

embroidered shirt and braided robe, he was in my eyes much more exotic than any beggar in rags, and I knew that it was useless to explain to this man that what I recognized in the other had nothing to do with appearances, or that indeed the whole value placed on sensory perceptions was undergoing a revolution in my mind. It was just as well that I did not try to express what was so clear but as yet inexpressible with the language I had, for the kindly man, steering me to the door of the mosque, invited me to attend a meeting of the fuqara that Thursday at his house. *Fuqara*, the plural of *faqir*, meaning "poor man," designates the followers of the Path in accordance with the Qur'an, which declares that truly we are poor and that He is the Rich, the Rich being one of the Divine Names. After my two extraordinary encounters in the streets of Nahb, the way I was invited to the Assembly of Fuqara was ordinariness itself, but I knew that it was the next inexorable step in a dance whose every move had been planned even before the musicians had gathered to play.

The Assembly of Dhikr, or Invocation, was held in a magnificent house that lay hidden in a little alley behind high walls. We entered through a heavy wooden door, stooping as we went through, to find ourselves standing in a wide courtyard filled with lemon trees surrounding an alabaster fountain that splashed clear water into an oval basin. At one end of the courtyard, in front of the salon, was a large area paved with marble. Divans had been placed in a wide circle on either side of the salon door, leaving a path down the middle for the fuqara to be served with glasses of hot mint tea during their recital. When we arrived the evening had already begun, and the fuqara were engaged in praising the Divine Creator. They would sing four lines, then chant the Divine Name, and then sing another four lines. Halfway through a song they would change both the Invocation and the melody. The hot, sweet tea was served from silver trays by other members of the Order, and somehow it in no way broke the concentration and devotional mood of the gathering. I was seated in one of the two circles without fuss and immediately joined in the Invocation, while taking in the spectacle around me. I saw that some were enormously intrigued by the impressive house and the arrivals of various members of the fuqara, that some were deeply involved in the singing and enjoyed the beauty of the songs and their own voices, but that others were in a state of deep concentration, as if completely alone. They sat cross-legged, their hands folded in their laps, their eyes shut. As they sang, they would occasionally look up, and I could see eyes misted with absorption. More than once, I saw a faqir discreetly wipe tears from his eyes. At one point, a man of about twenty seemed so overwhelmed that he could not contain what welled up within him. The others scrupulously left him alone, although I noticed that one very noble and ancient faqir moved over to sit beside him. Almost immediately, the tumult within the young man seemed to subside, even though the old man spoke not a word, nor did they exchange so much as a glance. They sang and sang through the night. My voice was hoarse with repeating the Divine Name, but they were far from the end of their resources. I did not really know how best to benefit from the experience, for although I tried to concentrate like the more experienced among the fuqara seemed to do, I was fascinated by the spectacle of the robed singers and the serving of the tea and the constant arrival of more fuqara. I longed to see the strange dervish of the market place once more and was sure that he would turn up. After about an hour of singing, the air shuddered with a voice that called out, "*Allahu akhbar*"—"Allah is greater"—three times. Every head turned to the door, and there he was, my dervish, staff in hand, barefoot. He was ushered into the circle opposite me with great reverence. He was like the chief of some primitive mountain tribe as he sat among the robed figures, who each bowed to him in turn. I longed for him to see me, but it was impossible, for he had been placed with his back to me. I nudged my companion to indicate that this was the man I had seen in the souks. If only he would look at me! I was sure that this would be a vital step on the way, although I had no basis for this strange conviction.

Song after song saw the moon vanish from our sight and the stars intensify their glow. The Invocation had filled me with a calm serenity without any emotional "color." If the tears that a faqir wept came from this peace, then they were not tears of grief or joy. But if not, from where did they come?

These thoughts were flitting through my all but thoughtless head when I was conscious that someone was standing directly behind me. I turned abruptly and looked up to see the dervish in his pointed cap towering above me. His ferocious face changed; the mask of sternness vanished. The eyes, misted with the Divine Name, glowed in his craggy skull, and his wrinkled face was suffused with a smile of tenderness and beauty the like of which, until that day, I had not seen. A moment later he was back in his circle, cross-legged and composed, singing as he had been before. I was overwhelmed with joy and glanced up at one of the fuqara who had seen the exchange. He nodded gravely his approval, then shut his eyes and went on singing. Something had happened. I could not tell what it was, but I knew it had happened. With the same immediacy that the body feels when an influenza virus is coursing through the bloodstream, I felt something present—in me. The singing continued for another hour.

At a certain moment, two thirds of the gathering departed, leaving about thirty people. Those who remained closed ranks into one circle and began chanting the Tahlil—"There is no god. There is only Allah." The dervish was on the opposite side of the circle to me, but he now seemed oblivious of the whole gathering, and his eyes were shut tight as he called out the Invocation. At a given signal, the group rose, and I realized that they were about to perform their sacred dance. I knew that such practices demanded initiation and wondered if I should leave the circle. However, they were so intent upon the dance that I felt I could remain with them, for even to have left the circle would have meant breaking the current of energy that I could already feel flowing through our clasped hands.

Six men stood beside the circle, singing the most ravishing counterpoint to the rhythmic invocation of the

dancers. It was scarcely a dance, but rather an invocation *expiri*
that used the whole body and was completely dictated by
the breathing that gave it rhythm. For what we later
reckoned was about half an hour, we continued our sway-
ing and dignified dance. The tempo changed and quick-
ened. I felt completely disembodied now. I was no more
than a gust of air that called upon the Living Lord. I had *ex*
lost all sense of being an observer or a stranger; I had
even begun to lose any sense of being a worshipper. I was
the flute, and the note passed through me. Suddenly, my
left hand was wrenched away from the man beside me.
Startled, I opened my eyes and saw beside me the wild
dervish. Sweat streamed from his brow, and his eyes
glowed dimly. He grasped my hand in his and rejoined
the circle. I felt what seemed like an electric shock surge
through my arm and up to my heart. I almost passed out,
then I recovered and tried to concentrate on the sacred
dance. A few moments later, the dance ended. The
fuqara sank to the ground where they were and shut their
eyes. Some mopped their brows.

From behind us a voice, silvery and pure, floated
across the marble courtyard. The Qur'an filled the air
and poured into our hearts like balm. Peace de- *ex*
scended upon us. A prayer was said, and it was time
to leave. The last image I had of the dervish was of
him disappearing ahead of us down the alley, on his
head an enormous plate of couscous, a gift from our
host to the holy man.

When we got back to the hotel, dawn was about
to break. We said the prayer, and although beyond fa-
tigue, fell into our beds and slept a deep and dream-
less sleep.

A few hours later, I awoke and went to the little café to have breakfast. I found my companion already there, and before he could say a word I launched into my plan. I had awoken with the firm conviction that a Shaykh of Instruction did exist and that we would discover him. I knew it. It was simply a matter of finding his address and setting out to visit him. This complete change in my attitude was without any basis, except that I was well aware it was bound up with what had happened during the sacred dance the night before. There was no way of proving or demonstrating this. The only proof of my certainty was to put it to the test. I saw that the patience of Othman, my companion, was at an end. He felt he had hung around in the city too long and that the time had come to continue the journey he had originally planned. I begged a favor of him. If I could find the address of the Shaykh that day, would he come with me to see him? Reluctantly, he agreed, insisting that this would be his last gesture before continuing on his way. Before he changed his mind, I dashed away to find the vital information.

I realized that I had no idea where to begin. What was I to do? Go into a mosque and ask, "Can you please give me the address of a spiritual master?" It was absurd. I had to be practical. Start at the beginning. Whom do you know in Nahb that you could ask? The imam. Yes, but he does not approve of such things and sees Islam only as a kind of strict club with ritual obligations a condition of membership—little to do with the Islam of the Prophet which I hopefully sought. A friendly and roguish antique dealer in the souks, whose small shop was piled high with fine velvet hangings and carved chests. He smoked hashish, but I had learned not to make hasty judgments about smokers. If he was a smoker, he was bound to know some venerable men. That was it!

I set out for his shop and arrived out of breath at the door to find him puffing contentedly on a long wooden pipe. He sat me down and ordered mint tea. We talked. He showed me a fine Qur'an in manuscript, which he lovingly kissed and held to his heart. I asked my question, and he immediately became excited. He sipped his tea. He frowned.

"No. I do not know of any Shaykh. I'm not a good enough man to know a thing like that. But I have a friend. He has made the pilgrimage. He would know. If anyone in Nahb knew, he would."

He clapped his hands, and his boy came to us. He sent him off to the house of his friend with instructions that the man should come to his shop at once. Ten minutes later, a lean old man with a gentle, smiling face came into the dark of the shop. The two men spoke in Arabic for about five minutes. The old man sat beside me.

"Yes. I know of two Shaykhs. One is right here in Nahb, but he is very weak, and I don't believe he takes disciples any more. The other is in Falah. His name is—"

I held my breath. "That is the one!" I exclaimed before he could even say the name. "This is whom I am seeking. Please, can you tell me where he lives?"

"If you return here in an hour, I will give you the address of his zawiyya.* He is a very holy man, a great

---

* *zawiyya:* literally, a corner; the house of a Shaykh and his disciples.

saint. Yes, I will find the address for you." He smiled contentedly and got up to go in search of the address.

Two hours later, we were driving toward Falah. We had little difficulty in finding the zawiyya, which lay on the edge of the medina behind a green door and a long passage like the entrance to any ordinary house. The inner doorway opened onto the mosque of the zawiyya, which was simple—white walls and rush matting on the floor—and filled with a serenity that permeated my whole body. It was just before sunset, and some of the fuqara had gathered for the sunset prostrations. They greeted us, squatted on the ground, and invited us to join their circle. We explained why we had come, and their faces showed disappointment.

"What a pity! You have missed him. Our Lord the Shaykh has gone to the capital. We don't know when he'll be back. We don't even know where he'll be staying there—if indeed he is still there. He travels all over the country, you see. What a pity!"

It had seemed that our quest was over; now it looked as if it had just begun. I saw Othman's face fall and knew he would not consent to another long journey with no guarantee of success at the end of it. What did I want to do? they asked. Go to the capital and try to find him, or wait for his return? I saw that Othman was about to withdraw from further involvement in my adventures. Perhaps he was right. Perhaps all this had nothing to do with me. Perhaps I shouldn't be roaming about searching for a master. Perhaps it was not meant. During the past weeks, I had avoided decisions, letting things happen as they might, and I was reluctant to make a choice at this crucial point.

"Let us say the Maghrib. After the prayer we will decide, Othman."

He agreed. The handful of fuqara lined up, and we made our prostrations. After the prayer, the oldest faqir, an imposing man with a distant smile like that of an aloof but friendly grandfather, told us that he knew now what had to be done. We were to meet him at the door of the zawiyya the next morning at five o'clock and he would take us to the Holy Shaykh. By leaving before dawn we would avoid travelling in the sweltering midday sun. Othman gave in. He too was now caught up in the excitement and mystery of our quest.

We were outside the zawiyya before dawn. The old man took us inside for the Fajr prayer. There were five fuqara in the mosque and they explained that several were travelling with the Master. After the *salat,* a long litany of different prayers was repeated by the fuqara, who sat in a close circle with eyes lowered. When the devotions were over, we said farewell and set out on our way. We were in high spirits and joined the faqir in singing invocations to the Lord. After about an hour, we arrived at a crossroads which pointed out the highway to the capital as being on the right, and on the left, a town called Si' Sliman.

"Left!" declared our guide.

We were both startled, but Othman obediently turned onto the left fork of the road and headed away from the capital. We checked with each other and agreed that, according to the sign, we were going the wrong way. Perhaps the road was up, perhaps this was the old road, perhaps we ought to ask. He could have made a mistake. No, he had not made a mistake. This was a "slight detour," which would permit him to visit his family in Si' Sliman. Our elation was still with us, and we laughed about it, agreeing that we should just let happen what had to happen and that it was all clearly out of our hands. So we stopped in the small town, had mint tea and dusty biscuits, did a lot of handshaking, and got back into the car.

Of course, by now the sun was quite high in the sky, and Othman complained that our dawn departure had been pointless. On we hurtled in the opposite direction from the capital. Next the old man informed us that we would turn back onto the highway at the next town. However, there was a faqir who would have more recent news of the Holy Shaykh than he had. It would be wise to stop at his house. In any event, it was certain he would know the exact location of the Shaykh's party in the capital. We gave up. We were clearly not going to get near the capital until that evening. Yes, we would stop at the villa of the local faqir. He dictated the lefts and rights until we came to a small white house with an enormous bougainvillea laden with crimson blossoms at its gate. No sooner had Othman parked opposite the house than its owner came running out to greet us, his hands waving above his head, his house robe billowing.

"Ah, what a pity! You have just missed our Lord the Shaykh. He left the house only a few minutes ago. He arrived unexpectedly, waited a little, and then departed. Never mind. He has gone back to the zawiyya at Falah. You will see him there. You might as well come in and have some mint tea."

So we had been on the right road after all! The old man beamed at us and tapped his heart with his forefinger, then pointed to the sky.

"Moulena!" he declared. "The Lord!"

We began to climb out of the car when another car swung around the corner and stopped a few yards away. The old man turned to us, his face overflowing with joy.

"He is here. Our Lord the Shaykh is here."

At that moment, a robed figure jumped out from behind the wheel of the car and waved to the old man. "I don't understand it," the chauffer called out. "He said we had to come back."

The door was opened, and a hand came out. The chauffeur grasped it, and a figure robed in a white djellaba and voluminous white burnoose stepped onto the road. It was the venerable Shaykh and Saint of Allah, my Master. I thought I was looking for him, and there, in that remote place, he had found me.

I shall not, cannot describe him. It would not be correct. It is enough to say that my Lord and Venerable Master was over a hundred years old—exactly how many, nobody seemed to know. His health—praise be to the Merciful Lord of the Universe!—was perfect. He performed the ritual prostrations each day in such a manner that we never ceased to be reminded of the glory of *salat* and of the humility it opens in the heart. He was the complete and perfect Muhammadan Man, the Shaykh of Shaykhs, the Pole of the Universe.

He received us in the small salon of the faqir's house. He sat in one corner of the room, cross-legged on the divan, his disciples seated about him. We were placed on his right-hand side. He welcomed us and inquired the purpose of our journey. He listened with courtesy beyond manners, with an attentiveness that was altogether radiant. At one point he sat in silence, utterly absorbed, withdrawn, bathed in the Divine Presence. Light poured from him and filled our hearts. My body temperature had risen considerably on approaching the Master, and it remained that way all through the interview. It was not uncomfortable, but I had a heightened awareness of every move I made and every gesture and glance of the Holy Shaykh. I inquired afterward about this strange heat I felt, and the faqir I asked seemed pleased and told me that this sometimes happened at such an encounter and that it was considered a good sign. He would say no more.

After another of these long and beautiful silences, in which we all basked as in sunlight, the Master told us we were to follow his car and return to the zawiyya as his guests. We kissed his hand and left his presence. A few minutes later, we were on our way back to Falah.

The guardian of the zawiyya greeted us at the door and showed us to the room Othman and I were to share. His turban, wound loosely around his head, was tilted low over his forehead. He had lost the sight of one eye and wore a cloth patch over it. The rest of his face was wreathed in a thick, curling beard and neatly trimmed mustache. When he smiled, there was a striking flash of white teeth and one shining eye that you saw. No more. He greeted us enthusiastically and told us what a blessing

it was that we had been led to our Lord the Shaykh.
Othman asked if there was any form of initiation. The
guardian nodded.

"Don't worry. You will be sent for when the time
comes. You have been accepted. You are here. You are
here."

During the next few days, the pattern of life at the zawiyya began to unfold. We rose at dawn for the Fajr
prayer, followed by the recital of the noble Wird of our
Shaykh. The Wird is a form of litany of Qur'anic ex-
cerpts, prayers, and *dhikr,* each repeated a specific number of times decided upon by our Master. The Wird was
the divine gift of the Lord to His most beloved saints and
provided a means of both spiritual protection and
spiritual advancement to the murid, or disciple. Following the Wird was the dawn recitation of Qur'an, and after
devotions came breakfast. At midday the fuqara ate together, and in the evening, at sunset, the Wird was again
chanted and Qur'an sung. After the evening prayer came
the evening meal and bed. On Thursdays, the fuqara met
in the evening and held assembly. Sitting together in a
circle, they sang the Diwan of the Venerable Shaykh and
then performed the Hadra, the sacred dance I had taken
part in in Nahb. For the Thursday gathering, the Master
would descend and lead the devotions. Sometimes he
would lead the Hadra, directing it from the center of the
circle and giving his *baraka*—blessing—to the practice.
The difference in the Hadra when he led it was astound-
ing. Both in sobriety and bliss, one felt the tremendous
spiritual energy that surged into the heart under his guid-

ance. It was the custom after the Hadra and the singing
of Qur'an for the Master to give a brief discourse inter-
preting the spiritual path to the disciples, using a Qur'an
passage as the basis of the teaching. It was not unusual
during these talks to see men weeping openly or discreetly according to their inner state, for the words of the
blessed sage entered directly into the heart, which had
already been prepared for the wisdom, or *hikmat,* by the
act of Hadra.

These gatherings were the principal *shaghal,* or
practice, of the fuqara, and of vital importance. One very
exalted disciple of our Lord the Shaykh said to me that
what was expected from a murid of our Master was
courtesy. I asked him to define this, and he replied,
"Courtesy means sitting cross-legged with the fuqara
singing the Diwan of Sayedina Shaykh."

It was during these sessions that, little by little,
the illusory layers of "identity" would fall away. It
was while the Diwan was sung, containing as it did
the whole spiritual teaching of the Prophet, the Path
from start to finish, the Goal itself made vividly plain,
that there would descend on the murid who was fa-
vored by his Lord a state of Presence, and he would
find the waters of the Ocean rise about him and en-
gulf him in the Mystery.

The more I attended the Assembly of Fuqara, the
more I became aware—but of things that were painful to
the point where it was all but impossible to remain there.
And then, blessedly, inexplicably, when it was not expected or sought for, came the gift, the inestimable, precious, sublime gift that only He may give.

The first discovery of these evenings was the staggeringly superficial nature of one's concentration. At first, everything distracted me—late arrivals, the tea ceremony, trivial curiosity, dreaming, discomfort, a multitude of insignificant things. Then my thoughts themselves. Over and above the fidgetting and restlessness of sensory distraction came the uncontrollable racing and wandering of the mind. Then came desire and will—forcing oneself to think of the Divine Name, consciously praying. This raised an even more insuperable wall between oneself and peace. But, imperceptibly, peace came. When the body was still and the mind concentrated and fixed, yet absorbed and unfocussed, with waiting over and yearning stilled, when resting in the words and sounds themselves, when carried by the Supreme Name, then and only then, with the silence and swiftness of a falcon descending, the heart would be snatched away in wonder and awe.

Assembly and Wird were the visible practices of the fuqara, and the *awqat,* or "times" set aside for *dhikr,* were the personal work one did alone. The *dhikr* was given individually by Sayedina Shaykh to the murid, according to his spiritual needs, as a doctor would prescribe two different doses of medicine to two separate patients suffering from the same disease. Each of us had a specific *dhikr* to do a specific number of times. When we did it depended entirely on our spiritual desire and energy.

The practice of *dhikr* is an essential spiritual practice of Islam, for the believer is called to *dhikr* throughout the Qur'an. Tirmidhi records a noble Hadith in which the Lord Muhammad—blessings and peace be upon him!—declared, "When you pass by the gardens of Paradise, stop and enjoy yourselves." On being asked what these were, the Prophet replied, "The Assemblies of *Dhikr*."

Abu Musa relates the Prophet as saying, "He who invokes his Lord and he who does not are like the living and the dead." Both Bukhari and Muslim transmit this Hadith in their collections. The science of the practice, with its specific numbers and the use of Qur'an and the Divine Names and Attributes, stems directly from the Prophet himself, Allah's peace and blessings be upon him! Abu Huraira relates this Hadith: "If anyone says a hundred times, morning and evening, 'Glory to be to Allah, and I begin with praise of Him,' only one who said what he said, or more than it, will bring anything more excellent than he on the Day of Resurrection." Both Bukhari and Muslim have transmitted this.

Within only a few days, I realized that I was learning my Islam from the fuqara. That is not to say simply that I deepened my understanding of the Qur'an and the rites and the Sunna in their company; it is to say that I learned how to live. I mean how to walk and how to sit and how to listen and when to be silent. I learned how to eat and how to refrain from food, how to wait and how to be still. Our Venerable Master had told us that in the stage we were at, there was no point in reading anything apart from the Qur'an. It was only as the days went by that the full meaning of the instruction became clear.

My first lesson in Tasawwuf was "breakfast." I liked my breakfast, and it was to me the most important meal of the day. It was simple enough—just tea (not mint tea), toast, conserve, and butter. That was all. For the fuqara, breakfast consisted of a cup of hot coffee followed by dry bread and, on some occasions, a thick soup followed by mint tea. This, I decided, was too much for my delicate stomach, and so when breakfast time came, I would slip out of the zawiyya and go to a little café in the town where they served the kind of breakfast I preferred.

The fuqara were most curious as to what happened to me in the mornings, and I was very defensive. On one occasion, as I set out, one faqir offered to come with me. I insisted on going alone. The next day, another faqir asked me about my breakfast. I made it clear that I didn't want them to worry about me and that I was quite happy. They, however, were not. I became angry and I insisted that there was nothing more reasonable than eating what one could and not forcing oneself to eat what would make one ill. In the middle of my sentence, the faqir broke into a song from the Diwan, and, to my frustration and inexpressible anger, the others joined in. I was seething with rage at what I felt was an injustice.

The next morning I was up before the others as usual in good time to slip out for my breakfast, but somehow I could not go. I loved the fuqara. Did a cup of tea mean that much to me? It came into my heart that it was my dependence on the ritual that bound me and not the physical objects of toast and black tea. I sat where I was, and when the time for breakfast came, I went and sat in the circle among the fuqara. They greeted me in their usual friendly way, making no reference to the fact that it was not customary for me to turn up for breakfast, but I could see that they were pleased. In a little while, breakfast was brought into the room. On the table was freshly baked bread, a large plate of butter, and a jar of thick, fruity conserve. They waited for me to open the meal. I broke the bread and passed it around. I raised mine to my lips and declared the Bismillah—"In the name of Allah." It was only later that I came upon the Hadiths that spoke against solitary eating when it could be avoided. Food, like prayer, was a blessing that increased as the number of participants increased. It was not long before I began to discover my dependency on food habits, about fantasy anxieties I had that I would not eat, about hunger itself—the hunger for food in the belly and hunger for food in the mind.

Abu Darda reported the Messenger as saying, "Provision searches for a man in the same manner as his appointed time." This is transmitted in *Al-Hilya* by Abu Nu'aim. Both Bukhari and Muslim record Abu Huraira's Hadith: "The Prophet said; 'Two people's food is enough for three, and the food of three is enough for four.'"

Al-Miqdam b. Ma'dikarab recounted hearing this from the Messenger: "No one has filled any vessel worse then a belly. Some mouthfuls to keep his back straight should be enough for the child of Adam, but if there is no escape, then let him fill it one third with food, one third with drink, and leave a third empty." Both Tirmidhi and Ibn Majah have transmitted this.

The same two tell of Umar b. al-Khattab recounting the following Hadith: "If you sincerely trusted in Allah, He would provide for you as He does for the birds who leave hungry in the morning and come back full in the evening."

So it was that in these early days at the zawiyya, the first thing that happened to me was the collapse of my digestive system. At supper one evening, in the blessed presence of our Master, I refused a very spicy dish. Sayedina Shaykh inquired as to my refusal. He was told of my complaint, and he looked at me for a long time, his eyes narrowed into a deep, affectionate laughter, and his face was lit by his incomparable smile. In the dazzling light of his laughter, it did not occur to me to question what was so funny about my gastric agony. Afterward, I realized something of its import. This was my disease. Had someone asked me of my faults, gluttony would not have figured on the list. The list might have been reprehensible, but not for a moment would I have admitted to being a glutton. It was something I had always associated with grossly fat people who overate. I began to realize that I had no idea how to eat, except in the way of our culture, which reflected my own fantasy involvement with satisfaction. With the fuqara, it was different. Not only did the meal begin with "In the name of Allah," but there was almost no conversation and I observed that the more developed murids ate little and avoided both appearing ascetic and obliging others to urge them to eat more. As always, the perfect model was Sayedina Shaykh. He scarcely ate at all, yet it seemed that he partook fully of each dish set before him. He did not speak during the meal, except to indicate when the next course should be placed before us. He ate with the same collected awareness with which he performed every act. His meal was a prayer as his prayer was a meal.

The life of the zawiyya was animated both by the

fairly regular community of the fuqara and by the visiting murids and fuqara who came from the desert and the mountains. Because of our Master's most exalted spiritual position, men of every spiritual station came to the zawiyya for his blessing or to be raised up in consciousness, by Allah's grace, to a higher station. Dervishes of every kind came to the door of the zawiyya and were all treated to the same friendly welcome. We soon learned to discern who were the *saaliheen,* the righteous ones—those whose bearing was most humble, whose presence was least felt, and whose silence was most profound. They were those beloved slaves of their Divine Lord who were most detached from men, most awed in the presence of Sayedina Shaykh, and most moved in their worship.

Among the fuqara, three men especially impressed by the purity of their lives. The enemy of man is himself —or rather that illusion of selfhood he experiences in the dream-state we call normal consciousness. In the terminology of Tasawwuf, the *nafs,* or "experiencing-self," is that illusory "I" that has to be polished away by the perpetual turning from it toward the Lord in *dhikr* until its true nature emerges, which is none other than the Ruh —the Spirit, which is pure Light. In these men, the *nafs* seemed but a fine film over a radiant otherworldly spirit, for there was very little of "them" left. They were devoid of "character." Some foibles remained, like small scratches on a smooth surface, and that was all. When they came into the mosque or a room at the zawiyya, they made no impact, except perhaps the vague sensation that the light had been imperceptibly turned up in the lamps.

I thought of my old colleagues and of those men Kasul had written about, and how massive was their "personality." They would bring any conversation to a halt when they entered a room, even if they did not speak. Their vibrations would clamor for attention, and their agitation would spill out on others, affecting the whole group. With the fuqara, it was the opposite. Their presence was a guarantee of calm, an antibody to agitation. An astonishing Hadith of Abu Huraira about these qualities tells of the Prophet saying: "The slave of the dinar, the slave of the dirham, and the slave of the silken coat are miserable. When one of them is given something he is pleased, but if he is not, he is displeased and disappointed. When thorns pierce him they cannot be extracted. Blessed is the man who sets the reins of his horse on the path of Allah, with wild hair and dusty feet. If he is guardian he does his duty, and if he is at the back of things he is contented there. If he asks permission to join a company it is not granted to him, and when he intercedes for someone not even that is accepted." This is in the collection of Bukhari. Such were the fuqara of Sayedina Shaykh.

Zirhouni was the muezzin of the zawiyya mosque. He was a small, bowed figure who seemed to walk in the perpetual *ruku* (second position of the *salat*), so bent was his back. His eyes were watery with age and tears. He had one winter djellaba and one summer one. He slept on a straw mattress in a corner of the mosque. He knew the Qur'an by heart, yet if the fuqara forgot it in recitation, he would never correct them unless his help was sought. It was rare to come upon him when he was not engaged in doing *dhikr* with his *tasbih*—beads—moving slowly through his fingers. I knew that he had been the muezzin for years, and I longed to know how he had come to serve our Lord the Shaykh. One day I found him alone in the mosque, and after a little talk—he was always concerned about my health—I asked him to tell me.

He sat silent for a while and looked at me almost reproachfully, as if I should not have asked him questions about something so valueless as his history. He sighed. Then he pointed to the sky with his forefinger in a gesture I had seen used often by the fuqara.

"Moulena." He repeated it, nodding. "The Lord." Then he began:

"It was twelve years ago that I became a faqir of Sayedina Shaykh. I lived in the little hillside town of the blessed saint whose descendant is our Master."

I nodded. It was his sanctuary that Othman and I had visited on our way to the zawiyya.

"I was married, children, worked as a tailor. In those days, I was not a dervish and did not attend the meetings of the local fuqara. I said my prayers and went to the mosque on Friday like any good Muslim. At Ramadan I kept the fast, on Idh I paid the *zakat.** One day I was walking through the lanes of the old town when I ran into my brother-in-law. He seemed delighted to see me, which surprised me, since normally we had very little to say to each other. He told me that the night before he

---

* *zakat:* the 2½ percent tax on possessions that every Muslim pays each year for redistribution among the community.

had had an amazing dream. He had been in heaven. It was radiant and shining. Angels and saints sang their praises of the Divine Creator. It was Friday, and he followed the angels to the Great Mosque. The mosque was made of white marble, its minaret a glittering diamond tower. He looked up as the call to prayer was made. And I was the muezzin, robed in white, light streaming from my body. The muezzin of Paradise. I told my brother-in-law that such an eventuality was most unlikely and that I would count myself lucky to escape eternal punishment. He seemed annoyed and insisted that it was a true dream.

"No sooner had he left me than I encountered an old friend, who was himself a dervish. He was a little surprised to see me in this back lane of the town, for I was precisely whom he sought. He told me that that same evening a very exalted saint and Wali Allah would be in the town. His disciples were meeting in the house of one of the local fuqara, and the Holy Master would be there to give a discourse and meet with the people. I told him this was very interesting, but that I didn't go out much. He insisted that I come, informing me that the moment he had heard of the saint's visit he had thought of me. In the end, to keep him happy, I agreed to go to the Assembly of the Fuqara.

"The courtyard was crowded, and there must have been about two hundred people present. I sat at the back somewhere out of the way, half behind a pillar. When the singing was over and the supper was about to be served, a faqir came and told me that the Shaykh had asked for me to be brought to his table. I realized this was a great blessing, but could not understand why the honor should be mine. I was seated next to him. As the food was being laid out, he leaned close to me and told me that the next day I was to go with him to his zawiyya, which was then in Nahb. He said I was to be the muezzin of his mosque and a faqir of Allah. I felt his *baraka*—his blessing—pour through my body. There was no question of disagreement. I was weeping and filled with a great sense of relief, as if my whole life had been a baffling puzzle and had in one move been solved.

"The next day, I went to the house where Sayedina Shaykh was staying, and he took me with him in his car to Nahb. I have been with him ever since. Twice during these years I have felt that I wanted to leave. I said not a word to anyone. Twice I got to the bus station and twice I came back here, I don't know why. And each time, on my return, I was sent for by Sayedina Shaykh, and he was waiting for me in his apartment, his table spread with food, smiling, thanking Allah, and filling my heart with peace. Parting does not matter. All of us here in this zawiyya will pray again together in Paradise."

Again he nodded. His eyes were shining with tears. From the outside, in the distance, came the Ezan. He looked at his watch. He rose and walked slowly to the center of the mosque, and from his frail, broken figure came the call—reverberant, broad, and majestic. His voice filled the air and soared out across the town, which lay drenched in the dying rays of the sun. Zirhouni, the muezzin of Paradise, was calling the saints and the angels to bow before their Lord. After him, I whispered, *"La ilaha il'Allah."*

In the Jami'al-Bayan is recorded this Hadith: "Truly, there are among my people men who rejoice openly at the extent of the mercy of Allah and weep secretly in fear of His punishment. They live on the earth, but their hearts are in heaven. They themselves are in this world, but their minds are fixed on the hereafter. They live in serenity and draw near to Allah through the means of His grace."

Of all the fuqara none was humbler or more devoted than the keeper of the zawiyya, Abd'Allah. The name means "Slave of God," and he lived up to this name. When he sat with the fuqara, it was impossible to catch his eye, for he sat always with his eyes lowered, and I never saw him raise them except in the presence of our Master and then only to gaze at him briefly. I say "eyes," but he had in fact lost one eye quite recently and wore a patch that somehow made the other eye all the more powerful.

He had all the menial tasks to do, but I never heard him complain. If he became irritated, it was a squall that blew away as quickly as it came, leaving everything clear and bright. He loved all the fuqara, and his profound feelings for his Master were a lesson to every murid who came to the zawiyya.

One murid, a student from Nahb, asked him what he might do to please Sayedina Shaykh, and his reply was one word, *"Dhikr!"* I tried several times to get him into conversation, but each time I ended up doing some task around the zawiyya—brushing the carpets or fixing a door. His business sometimes seemed like a reproach, and one day as I sat in the mosque he kept passing me on some errand, his sleeves rolled up and his face covered in sweat. I asked if there was any work I could be doing. He went directly to the cupboard and unlocked it. He rummaged in a box and then came over and put in my hands a set of *tasbih*. Then, taking the beads in one hand, he moved them through his fingers calling out, "Allah, Allah, Allah, Allah, Allah," and he clenched his fist and shook it as if to emphasize the importance of his advice.

The imam of the zawiyya mosque was a delightful man. Aloof and fastidious, handsome in a princely manner, he was a model scholar, though in a totally different tradition from our own. His apartment was lined with manuscripts and books, and it seemed that there was no treatise on Tasawwuf he had not read and no commentary on Qur'an he did not know. He was Hafiz* of the Qur'an and could not only recite it, but could place an *ayat*† within seconds of hearing it. Obviously, as imam to Sayedina Shaykh, who was considered the *aalim* of the *ulama*,‡ as well as being a great saint, he was not only schooled in the best school, but had lived surrounded by men of learning and men at every stage of the spiritual journey. Yet never did he flaunt his learning. Indeed, I saw him keep silent at times when another man would have been driven to discourse, and he knew when speech was superfluous.

> *i.e., knew the whole of the Qur'an by heart.
> †*ayat:* Literally, a form; one verse of the Qur'an.
> ‡*aalim* (plural *ulama*): a scholar, a man of knowledge.

During my first weeks, I pressed him again and again to talk to me about Tasawwuf, but he would always decline. One eveing, we were invited to his study to take tea with him. He was in an expansive mood, and it seemed a good moment to try once more. I asked him point-blank for a definition of Tasawwuf. I felt that this would get him started, but he merely paused a moment in reflection and then said simply:

"Tasawwuf is loving the Lord and being kind to all his creation, even to insects."

That was all, and he went back to the ritual of preparing the mint tea.

Abu Dharr recounts a Hadith of the Messenger that declares: "To be present in the circle of a learned man is better than prostrating oneself in prayer a thousand times or visiting a thousand sick men or witnessing a thousand funerals." And so we sought his company and patiently waited, hoping he would begin to teach us, but, apart from Qur'anic exegesis and correcting points of detail in our prayer rites, he was not forthcoming. I even studiedly examined his extensive library and pointed to the vast tome of Ibn Arabi that he had filled with markers. He nodded and observed that these books contained secrets of the Unseen such as existed in no other book of the Science. He added that we should remember that he wrote nothing that had not been revealed to him in vision.

"There is nothing abstract there as far as he is concerned. No theory. Just description."

I begged him to tell me about these descriptions of the Shaykh al-Akhbar, but he merely said, "You will see for yourself. Do the work that Sayedina Shaykh has given you, and if it is Allah's will, very soon a door will open for you.'' And he graciously poured us another glass of mint tea.

It was in the nature of life at the zawiyya that the kind man who had corrected my prayer in the mosque at Nahb should turn up in Falah just when I needed him. Of course, he was a disciple of our beloved Master and smiled without the slightest vibration of surprise when he saw me among the fuqara. Although I was the last person to be able to measure what was happening to me, I supposed I was coming to the end of the first phase of my new education, and with every day the process seemed to be more difficult. I began to find the company of the others suffocating, and even Othman became intolerable to be with, partly because he was going through the same mutation. Each time I tried to be by myself, I would find one of the fuqara by my side. If I rose to slip out quietly, I would be asked my purpose, and no sooner did I suggest I wanted to take a walk than a faqir was designated to accompany me. Whatever excuse I made, I could not be alone. I began to intensify my search for solitude, but on the rare occasions when I managed to break free, I found my mind was so seething with the sense both of suffocation from the others and triumph at being alone that the times were over before I had done any of the spiritual work that I told myself I was being kept from performing. I wanted to meditate, but how could I possibly do that when I was perpetually being interrupted with the most trivial chatter? I wanted to do *dhikr,* but how could I embark on a long session when my concen-

clerk

tration would inevitably be shattered by steaming glasses of mint tea and more conversation?

I began to examine the other members of the zawiyya most critically. I wanted solitude and contemplation. I decided they desired nothing better than idle talk and large meals. I was the spiritual man surrounded by shortsighted men unworthy of the great privilege of attending the court of the spiritual king. In this way, I reassured myself as I feverishly nursed my solitary moments snatched from the daily round of communal prayer and food that was zawiyya life.

It was in the middle of this tacit battle to gain what I considered my rightful privacy that the kind old Nahbi arrived. After greeting me, he sat down beside me, smiling broadly.

"Well, are you finding it difficult?" he asked.

"No," I replied, rather too hastily.

"Ah!" came his answer, as if it had been wrong of him to think such a thing.

The silence demanded filling, and I blurted out, "Why? Should I be finding it difficult?"

He smiled again. "No. It's just that some murids find it a little difficult at the beginning—a little . . . suffocating."

My heart was beating fast with gratitude. It was hard never being alone, but I had to be patient. That was it! I couldn't expect everyone to be of the same spiritual ambition as myself.

He put his hand on my arm. "I found it difficult, too."

That was all I needed, and I poured out my complaints to him. I blamed the fuqara, I blamed the culture for covering over the pure teachings of the Path, togetherness, tribal fear of the solitary . . . But the more I talked, the more I realized that somewhere I had got things radically wrong. Slowly, my talking ran down, the battery spent.

"And what do you do when you are by yourself?" The moment he asked me the question, I saw what had happened, but I tried to justify myself. No, I had not prayed or done *dhikr,* but that could only be done once a pattern had been established. There should be a place for *dhikr.* There, that was it!

The old man shook his head firmly, just as he had done once before in the mosque. No, I was wrong again.

"The Prophet—blessings and peace be upon him as long as men seek the Divine Presence—has said, 'Satan is with the solitary.' To be truly alone means just that. And you, when you are by yourself, are you alone? No. A thousand thoughts accompany you, a hundred *nafs*— your anger, your pride, your everything." He was laughing at me, but with such sweet understanding that I bowed my head in shame. "The struggle is not over yet. After it is over, you will see. You have to work very hard to be alone. That comes later. When you are able to be alone, you will find that you *are.* You won't have to fight for it. To be alone, correctly, according to the Wisdom, you must first learn to be with others. Don't fight. Look at your Shaykh! Look at your Shaykh!"

He folded his hands across his lap and lowered his eyes. "*Abd.* Slave. This is Islam. This is the Path. This is Peace." He shut his eyes and sighed deeply. He folded his hands again in his lap and sat in complete stillness. I did not move, and I realized that my whole body was tense. I was uncomfortable and felt I should not move, but I began to get cramp in my toes, so I shuffled into a more comfortable position as best I could and began to do my *dhikr* silently. Eventually, I shut my eyes as well. No one disturbed us, and around us all was deep silence. After some time, I opened my eyes, my heart fluttering like a trapped bird. Eventually, the old man too opened his eyes. "Allah!" He exhaled the word slowly and then he turned his gaze upon me. He nodded solemnly. "It takes time. It takes time."

The others began to arrive for the sunset prayer.

One of the mysteries of Assembly, revolving as it were around the central mystery of the descent of the Divine Presence on particular members of the circle, was the mystery of where we found ourselves. Something that is true of every moment in our lives became impressively manifest in Assembly. Each person was exactly where he should be. It seems odd put like that, but it is precisely my meaning. One's nearness to Sayedina Shaykh, the person on one's left and on one's right—all of these seemed to measure one's place in the cosmos with exactness. In the early days of sitting with the fuqara, I had found myself placed either beside or very near the Master. At that time, I was often embarrassed by the fuss that was made because I was a foreigner, and I longed to slip invisibly into a corner and get on with the business of Invocation, and while it was an immeasurable honor to be seated beside the Master, it deprived me of the joy of seeing him, which I could only do by turning around.

Then, imperceptibly, and later markedly, as I became ill at ease among the fuqara, I found that I was slipping away from the Master. Meeting by meeting, I moped away from him, as if I were edging toward the door. Where once I had sat with venerable and developed murids on either side of me, I now found myself with novices from whatever villages we visited, or with the ones who served the couscous at the end of the gathering. Eventually, I found that I was almost out of the room altogether, utterly distracted by my companions on either side. I was miserable. The more I tried to get near to Sayedina Shaykh, the more mysteriously I would find myself pushed aside, out of the way of everything. To make matters worse, it seemed to me that the sublime detachment of my Master had become a kind of specific disdain of my personal dilemma.

I recall talking with Othman after our first meeting with our blessed Master. I confessed to Othman that I had been astonished at his complete acceptance of me. "I kept expecting to be told I was a naughty boy," I admitted, and Othman laughed. "How funny!" he said. "And I kept expecting to be told I was a good boy!"

And now here I was needing some kind of guidance and receiving none. I was neither approved nor disapproved. I was not taught. I was told nothing. I just had to get on with it, and "it" was nothing less than the whole business of being me. And it was precisely "me" who was giving all the trouble. Loss of self was all very well, I mused, but the more I went on, the more of me there seemed to be! The *nafs*—

reading about it and talking about it were one thing, but the day was another.

Our gathering that Thursday was in the house of a poor workman in a block of new, crumbling flats, with children screaming on the stairs. The fuqara arrived with Sayedina Shaykh, he preceded as usual by the Qur'an singer, who sang out above the din of the neighbors to announce the arrival of the saint. There was a large gathering, and the townsfolk crowded in to catch a glimpse of the Blessed Master. The sight of these poor and undernourished people, gazing with such love and awe upon our Master, was moving, and I slipped into the background as they pushed forward to kiss his hand and receive his blessing. Eventually, the chanting of his Diwan began, and we all settled down. I was wedged in one corner of the L-shaped living room, completely out of sight of the Holy Shaykh, and on my right was a particularly heavy man who rocked against me as he sang, so that I could not concentrate for the rhythmic pulping of my ribs, while on my left was an overfriendly little boy, who insisted on beaming at me every time my glance moved around the room.

In the end, I gave up trying to create any kind of ambience of worship around me. I knew it was wrong to stop singing, for that made one merely use the singing as an emotional background to the *nafs'* own involvement, so I simply sang as best I could and kept my eyes lowered, undisturbed by the endless flux of tea servers and late arrivals. In a way, my physical discomfort was so acute that it acted as a block to my other distractions, and I ended up with both knees tucked in front of me, a position that hardly seemed to accord with regular breathing, contemplation, and Invocation.

I was just one crushed lump of humanity among about a hundred more, singing the night out in a city slum. That's all I know. For then it happened. I had done nothing. I was engulfed. Or had I overflowed? Both. My center was out there in the room, filling every corner of it. Or perhaps it was that I began where my fingers and my toes and my face ended and everything else began. Only a blurred contact held me to my body. My senses were gone. I could see—just, and hear—distantly, feel— perhaps. What was left of me was filled with an unbearable poignancy. I wept. My tears had to do with these people, yet I did not weep "for" them. Nor did *I* weep. A sluice gate had opened, and the river flowed. I had not given the order, I had not carried it out. I was the earth on which the teardrops fell. The fragment of me that remained knew to wipe its eyes and avoid observation. This I did, and I faintly grasped that the others were unaware that I had fallen from the great liner of their company and been rushed out in the wake of their engines to float in a fathomless ocean.

The singing was over, and it was time for supper. I stared fixedly in front of me, hoping, with what little brain remained to me, that I would be left undisturbed, when a faqir appeared standing over me. He bent down. All around, men were herding people into groups and putting out the tables for supper. He took my arm and raised me to my feet. I could no more protest than resist. As he guided me across the room, I wiped my eyes. He whispered in my ear that I was to sit at the table of Sayedina Shaykh.

The moment I got to the table, I knew that I was safe. He looked at me, and it was as if he nodded, but he made no such sign. He motioned me to sit down between two strange disciples, one of them an old mountain man with a grizzled beard and deep eyes, strong and fragile with years. I sat among them, dazed, unable to hear the conversation, but no longer worried that people would bother me. I could not have spoken had I wanted to, but everyone continued as if I were not there. I felt the occasional glance of our beloved Master take me in as he looked around his disciples, but no more than that. I was still afloat on a sea of such sweetness and bounty that it filled my whole body without drowning me, so that I floated like a cork, saturated but unsinkable.

The meal began. No one pressed me to eat, as had previously been the case, and when a piece of food was placed in front of me, I ate it, as was the custom, with a whispered *"Bismillah!"* During the meal, I felt a tremendous warmth grow in me for the old man at my side. It was not affection; it was something richer and more solemn, something sacred. I did not think, for my thinking apparatus was suspended, but from my new consciousness, which moved moment by moment, it came to me that as I was fed, so too I must share with this man beside me. I took from the large bunch of grapes on the table the finest, rosiest grapes I could see and placed them before him, whispering the Divine Name. No sooner had I done this than the hand of Sayedina Shaykh moved across the table and placed in mine what seemed even larger and more perfect grapes. I looked up at him and took the grapes. He gazed at me, and in the depths of that look, I saw. Everything connected in my mind. A flash, a tremendous, stunning second that must have been filled with angels' voices, and the man beside me and the room and the poverty and the table and grapes given and grapes received were unified in that blessed, blessed moment that lies forever beyond any words, as indeed does every moment of our lived existence, waking and sleeping. Sayedina Shaykh sat back on his divan, a task among so many accomplished, while I remained unmoving beside him, gently drifting to the shore, but changed, never to be the same again. The meal was over.

There was no greater sign of the unbridled power of the *nafs* than the effect of my experience at the Assembly of Dhikr. Rather than rendering me humble and setting me on the Path with renewed desire, it flung me into a tumult. Something tremendous had happened, and no description can do more than hint at the *idea* of what it was that had happened, and in my awareness of that fact, I waited to be sent for by our Master and for him to seal for me that mysterious event.

There was, however, not a sign from the Murshid. He was busy every day with visiting disciples, and I waited in vain for some sign of his recognition. The bubbling and smoking in the crucible of my *nafs* must have been awful, and recording it here I hesitate before setting it down, yet my ignorance and sense of false self-importance are no less than those of any man, and I decided that if I could not win the attention of my Master by my presence, that I must do so by my absence. The next evening, another Assembly of Dhikr was called. Feigning exhaustion, I asked the fuqara not to wait for me but to go on alone. I insisted that the last few days had been too charged for me and that I wanted to be by myself and absorb what had already happened. Disturbed, and after much protestation, the fuqara set out without me. No sooner had they gone than I was filled with self-reproach, then with self-pity. I went into the town for a walk—that apparently precious thing I had striven for which now seemed worthless. I sat down in a café and, like a spoiled child, ordered tea and an expensive cake. I had just started to gorge myself when I was joined by a student whose father attended the assemblies. He talked and talked, and I scarcely needed to make an effort to create the semblance of dialogue. The unfortunate student made me think again of Kasul, for he was everything the Librarian feared for "the educated man." His conversation was like a scrambled tape of media-fed information and consumer data. I listened appalled. Here he was in the town of the most venerable sage of his time, the source and fountainhead of knowledge, and he was utterly oblivious to it. His pathetic value judgments, based on ignorance and a smattering of false information, had made him turn from this learning as if it were some primitive superstition. It was not that he was in any way an exception to the cream of our developed educational process, simply more obviously devoid of any useful life-knowledge, crippled with opinions, his hostilities channelled into social concern, and his sheer existential panic tranquillized by a lust for consumer "stuff" that would never be assuaged.

Thrilled to have a visitor from one of the "developed" areas, he insisted that I go back to his "studio" and have supper with him and his wife, a teacher at the local school. It was all so disastrously correctly timed that I knew I had to accept and taste the full extent of my own stupidity. The studio was a small one-room apartment completely dominated by a shining white refrigerator that stood across one corner of the room like a household god. They almost bowed to it as they passed it, and it was opened and shut at least twenty times while they prepared the meal. I was glad they put the videometer on and forced me to watch their filmed antics of people prancing among the technological idols and listen to their endless imitative music.

The boy's wife was more touching than he, for she was torn between the powerful brainwashing of women that her culture inflicted on her and the impossible demands that living their new consumer life demanded of them. Their discontent was depressing, their longing to live the ideal reward-life that was fed to them by their videometer was desperate. I wanted to tell them that only a few miles away the Axis of the Universe, the Light of Muhammad, sat in glory, surrounded by poor but contented men who asked nothing of life, only knowledge of Allah. Yet I was with them, eating their plastic food, and not with the Venerable Master partaking of the mystical feast of life, nor had I the peace in my heart that could spill out and transform their unhappy household into a place of light and joy.

What was I doing there? I was filled with shame. I could not be cruel and tell them that the life they yearned for was poverty itself and that the poverty they feared was enough for life. I could not give them what they yearned for, for I had not gained it to give. My place was with my Shaykh, that I might begin to learn and understand the first vital displacement of my experiencing *nafs*. And all I had done was run away.

The evening over, I went back to the zawiyya and slipped under my blanket. There were about seven men stretched out along the walls of the large room, and my determination to rise and spend that night in *dhikr*, as the Master suggested we should, seemed impossible. But the driving force in me that longed for one step to be taken gave me no peace. If I could not do my *dhikr* in the room, then I would go out onto the flat roof and do it there. I would spend the night in *dhikr* outside the apartment of Sayedina Shaykh. I was not testing him and yet, in my heart, I was convinced that in the awesome state of his inner existence, he could not fail to know that his raw disciple watched the night at his door. I had been told that the Master did not sleep at night, or if he did, it was no more than a couple of hours.

Everyone was fast asleep when I tiptoed out onto the roof with my blanket and prayer rug. In the apartment of the Master I could hear the movement of one of his wives and the faint murmur of voices, then her departure. The lights remained on, but from within the room all was silence. I made myself comfortable against the wall and began to do my *dhikr* silently. At first, I was like a spy waiting breathlessly for a movement and secretly longed-for discovery, but it did not come. Slowly, as the stars moved across the sky, I succumbed to a sense of ease and sweetness. It seemed that to sit beside my beloved teacher with only a wall dividing us and to recite the Divine Name was a gift that could not be surpassed. And finally, even that contentment glided away, and all that was left was the vibrant immediacy of the Divine Name over and over in my heart.

The next thing I knew, it was dawn. I had not slept, but the night had passed, and my solemn task had been turned into a delight that ended all too soon. I said my dawn prayer with the *wudhu*—ritual washing—that had served for my night prayer, and no one seemed remotely aware of the vigil I had begun in such a tumult of feeling. One thing that the night had brought me was a light heart, and all the self-obsession of the days before had vanished. On being asked if I felt better, I asked hopefully if there was to be another assembly that night.

During breakfast, Sayedina Shaykh's chauffeur came in and told me to come at once to the Master. Overjoyed, I dashed out to the front of the zawiyya, where he sat in his car waiting for me. I knelt by the side of the road and kissed his hand. He smiled down at me with his overflowing love and his deep inner laughter that radiated understanding. He called me by my name and looked at me, holding my gaze and never ceasing from his gentle, almost imperceptible laughter.

"You must be careful at nights. You'll catch cold!"

With a small wave of his hand, he motioned me to get into the car behind him. I fell into the seat and a minute later was all but oblivious to the other two fuqara who tumbled in beside me. We sped off into the hills on another of our Master's mysterious visits to one of his murids, but I had no idea what route we took, for my heart overflowed with the joy of his love, which so purely refused to bind me to him, and yet, while fastidiously avoiding dependency on him, turned my heart to utter dependency on the Lord of the Universe, to whom all praise belongs.

There were many visitors to the zawiyya, and I was already able to get from some a vibrancy of spiritual quality that simply did not exist in the world from which I had come. I once observed to the guardian, Abd'Allah, that a certain visitor who had come for an audience with Sayedina Shaykh had moved me by his humility and dignity. The guardian nodded in affirmation.

"The *saaliheen*," he said and went about his endless tasks.

One morning I sat in the *minzah,* the meeting room of the zawiyya, studying the Diwan of our Master, when there came into the room a man who by his robes was clearly a desert nomad. His high, coiled turban crowned a young and handsome head; his face was bronzed from the wind, and he had a black, curling, pointed beard. He came in and saluted me gravely. He gestured to be given the *qibla*—the direction—and then turned to face it in prayer. After his prostrations, he rose and sat opposite me, his lips moving in silent *dhikr.* There came from him that serenity that the most exalted of the master's murids seemed to project, although it could be sensed more subtly than any projection, which would be active and thus of the *nafs,* not of the spirit; rather it hung around them in the way that musk makes its presence felt.

After a while, I addressed him hesitantly, and he

answered me with courtesy and brevity. I turned the conversation to our Master, for I longed to hear this man's appreciation of him. His face immediately lit up, but he spoke only of those qualities that I already knew and loved. I pressed him to tell me more about him to tell me stories. He smiled.

"The miracles. Yes, there have been many miracles. Make no mistake. He is the one. He is the one. He is the one. But not because of miracles. We are still impressed by the world of the senses, eh? Manifestations, events, yes, but the real miracle is hidden, invisible, not of time and space. Our Lord the Shaykh—he does nothing, hmm? He sits up there in his apartment wrapped in the Divine Presence. He seems to do nothing, but look at the activity that emanates from that stillness. You are here, and I am here, and there are many, many more who come and go and are transmuted. But he does nothing. He is . . . gone. You see, when he speaks, he speaks by Allah and for Allah. When he moves, it is by Allah and for Allah. He is a clear mirror which reflects only the Divine Presence. He is the perfect slave of his perfect Lord. He is the Nur-i-Muhammadi, the Light of Muhammad. If you knew what that was, eh? Look." He leaned over, picked up the small glass and the jug that were on the low table beside him, and held up the glass.

"Every object has consciousness of itself. Let us say that this glass . . . has consciousness of itself. It is able to know—up to there. Then it is full, yes? Now, this jug has consciousness of itself. It can know . . . up to here. But this glass cannot know what the jug knows. It can contain no more than its form allows. But look. This . . . can fill this."

He lifted the jug and poured the clear water until the glass overflowed. My thoughts flashed to the night of the meal with Sayedina Shakh. The man smiled and nodded, as if he knew my thoughts. He sat back among the cushions and sighed, *"La ilaha il'Allah."* He seemed to be examining me, but his face remained relaxed and his eyes were warm.

"Do not get lost in the thinking you have been taught. Psychologism!" (He said the word with great scorn.) "Influences, trance states, ecstasies . . . I have read how they try to explain away with words a science that begins where language ends. The beginning of the matter is wonder. Allah!" (He said the Supreme Name so that its second syllable hovered in the air, his voice filled with awe.) *"La tudrikuhu al absar wa huwa yudriku al absar, wa huwa al-Latifu al-Khabir.* He cannot be reached by vision, but He can reach vision, and He is the All-penetrating, the All-knowing. *La ilaha il'Allah.* One. The vessels are different; the water is the same. The lamps are many; the light is one. How do we know *La ilaha il'Allah* is true? *Muhammad Rasulullah.* Muhammad is the key. Muhammad, blessings and peace be upon him!"

He rose and came to where I was sitting, and I could see that he was filled with love. It pulsed in him like the light of a glow-worm. He sat beside me, and his voice became softer, almost secretive.

"And who is the Prophet? Ah! We are in awe of the spiritual state of our Lord the Shaykh. Imagine. Try, if you can, to grasp the mystery of the Blessed Messenger. Qur'an tells us to approach the mystery of Allah by recourse to His names and His attributes. Look at the sky, look at the stars, the ocean, and the mountains. How you are born and die and live your life and are fed—all this points to the mystery. I cannot know your essence—only your attributes, your thinking and willing and seeing and speech. This points me to the essence. Sayedina Muhammad.

"Who *was* our Prophet? Who was this man who brought an army to a halt to tend to newborn puppies and posted a guard that no harm would come to them? Who was this commander who instructed his chiefs to exert care as they rode, so as not to disturb the anthills? Mu-'adh b. Jabal tells of his saying, 'Those nearest to me are the pious, whoever they are and wherever they are.' Ahmad transmitted it.

"There was never food in his house for the following day, and he lived on barley bread and a handful of dates. He fasted much and slept little. Ibn Mas'ud told that the Messenger slept on a reed mat and rose with the marks of it on his body, so he said, 'Messenger of Allah, order us to spread something out for you,' and he replied, 'What have I to do with the world? In relation to the world, I am just like a rider who shades himself under a tree, then goes off and leaves it.' Tirmidhi, Ahmad, and Ibn Majah transmitted it. 'Do not consider any act of kindness insignificant,' Abu Dharr relates his saying in Muslim's Collection, '—even meeting your brother with a cheerful face.' His blessed and saintly wife, Aisha—peace be upon her—! told of his saying, 'The world is the dwelling of him who has no dwelling and the property of him who has no property.' Ahmad and Baihaqi both record it.

"Do you begin to see what perfection of humility was his?" He sat back, and I saw that his eyes were shining with unshed tears.

"This is the Master our Master loves. 'Every building is a misfortune for its owner, except what cannot, except what cannot . . .' Anas told this, and Abu Dawud transmitted it. This is Islam. You see how precious it is. It is not the thing that colors whole countries on the map —so many hundred million Muslims. No, no. If that were true, there would be no problem. Abu Dharr, that holy man, the Wise Companion, says that he told us, 'When one of you becomes angry when standing, he should sit down. If the anger leaves him, fine. If not, lie down.' Tirmidhi has collected this. Do you see? Do you grasp it yet? Abu Huraira tells of his saying, 'I have been sent to perfect good character.' That is in the book of Malik. You see now? *That* good character is none other than the Mystery of the mysteries. That is what it is all about,—Islam, this place, Sayedina Shaykh. That is Tasawwuf. Ibn Abd'Allah al-Ansari records him as saying, 'Do not attend the circle of any learned man except him who would call upon you to relinquish five things in favor of five others, namely:

to relinquish doubt in favor of belief,
hypocrisy in favor of sincerity,
worldliness in favor of asceticism,
pride in favor of humility,
enmity in favor of love.'

"This is Muhammad, Ahmad, the Praiseworthy, Mustapha, the Chosen One, our Lord and Prophet, the

Perfect Man who said, and it is Sayedina Ali—peace be upon him!—who has preserved it:

> 'Meditation in Allah is my capital.
> Reason and sound logic are the root of my existence.
> Love is the foundation of my existance.
> Enthusiasm is the vehicle of my life.
> Contemplation of Allah is my companion.
> Faith is the source of my power.
> Sorrow is my friend.
> Knowledge is my weapon.
> Patience is my garb and virtue.
> Submission to the Divine Will is my pride.
> Truth is my salvation.
> Worship is my habit.
> And in prayer lies the coolness of my eye and my peace of mind.' "

That was the substance of my meeting with the Muqaddim* from the desert who came and awakened in me my first knowledge of the Messenger—all blessings and divine peace be poured upon him and his companions and his family forever! Amen.

At last, I began to settle down to the life of the zawiyya without being engaged in a perpetual struggle. Slowly there grew in me a warmth and affection for these people whose sole happiness was to sit together and invoke the Name of the Beloved with such ecstasy and calm. Affection condensed and solidified into love, and I began to understand the underlying wisdom of the Prophet's Hadith that Abu Huraira retold in Muslim's Collection:

* *Muqaddim:* the deputy of a Shaykh.

"You will not enter Paradise until you believe, and you will not believe until you love one another. Let me guide you to something in the doing of which you will love one another: Salute all and sundry among you."

At long last, I began to follow the instruction of the Master—for he never ordered his murids, but rather gave them spiritual work which they could then carry out when the *himma,* or spiritual yearning, was awakened. So, too, I began to discover the true nature of *dhikr.* Dhikr, the Invocation of a Divine Name, was beginning to yield its secrets. The contrary states of concentration and absorption began to unite in the *Shaghal,* or practice, which is the state of fixity of attention and the state of being absorbed, the first being like the cat watching the mousehole and the second like seaweed yielding to the pull of the tide. Qur'an itself was *dhikr,* being the direct Divine Message revealed through the Angel, and the more one surrendered to its power, the more it unveiled its secrets to the listener. There are many instances of men dying in a state of serene bliss while hearing the Qur'an recited, and it was quite usual among the fuqara for its recital to be the divine means of opening a faqir's heart to knowledge, and the tears would flow.

The weeping of the fuqara must not be thought of as an emotional release in the sense of a zone of disturbed experience as measured by psychologism, for that is altogether different. The weeping that comes upon the faqir is not from the *nafs,* but rather from the *qalb,* the heart. The heart is that faculty by which man experiences his true nature and the nature of reality. The weeping of the faqir is the removal of a veil from the heart. This is not his doing; it is the Lord's. Yet it is none other than he who makes the tears flow. This is why the Prophet— blessings and peace be upon him!—said, "Weep, and if you are not able to weep, imitate weeping, that, by Allah's grace, you will be able to weep." Thus the surrendering of the *nafs* begins.

I soon realized why it was that when a faqir wept he was discreetly left to himself, then obliged to say the ritual prayer, if it was the time for it. To comfort him would be to rouse the *nafs* and mingle the griefs of the *nafs* with the roused and responsive *qalb*. So also, if it was the time of the *salat*, the prayer itself would both deepen the state of the murid and cleanse it of the incrustations of the *nafs*. In all these matters, the fuqara manifested a sobriety that was the fruit of their discipleship with our Master, and never once was there any display of hysteria, of trances, or of psychic states of excitement.

One morning, when the zawiyya was quiet, I determined to practice *dhikr*. I had been brought a cup of coffee and some bread for breakfast, and when the boy came to take away the tray I asked him for another cup of coffee. He shrugged and said that there was none left in the pot and that there was no one in the kitchen to make any. He left me, and I settled down to perform the *dhikr* I had been given. I had not got very far when I found that my mind was straying back to that cup of coffee. The boy was surely very lazy! If not, then it meant that the household really couldn't be bothered to prepare even a pot of coffee. Once more, I was sinking in the mire of these illusory needs which had so little to do with their actual "form"—the short-lived stimulation of some coffee. My complete breakfast fantasy, if you like, still lingered in that cup of coffee, which my desire still nursed with such tenacity. I tried to recommence my *dhikr,* but it was useless. I sat there depressed and irritated, both with myself and the zawiyya. I heard nothing, but I knew before he appeared that he was coming toward me, just as a surging wave on the shore indicates the arrival of a great ship. I sat up, pretending I was doing my *dhikr.* Sayedina Shaykh—may Allah be pleased with him!—stood in the doorway. In his hand he held a steaming glass of coffee.

I started to rise, but he motioned me to sit down. He came to me and placed the glass in my hand. *"Bismillah!"* As he pronounced the blessing, his eyes looked deep into my heart. He then crossed the room and sat opposite me while I sipped the hot drink, my heart pounding. He paid no more attention to me, but seemed to sink into a deep absorption in the Divine Presence, so that he became more radiant and more awesome by the moment. Light poured from him and spilled out, filling the room with serenity. I finished the coffee and whispered the thanksgiving, *"Al-hamdulillah",*—"Praise belongs to Allah." The exalted Master took his black *tasbih* and began silently to invoke the Divine Name. I lifted mine, and in his blessed company I recommenced the *dhikr* with a clear heart.

During the next few days, the zawiyya stirred to a new activity and excitement. It was preparing for the Moussem of the Prophet, celebrating his birthday, and for the one that followed immediately after it—

the Moussem of our Beloved Master. I was told that
the latter was a tremendous event and that it was an
opportunity for spiritual enrichment, for soon the zawiyya would be pulsating with the energy of the most
exalted believers, planets circling in the orbit of the
Sun, our Shaykh. I knew, too, that the Moussem was
to signal the end of my time among the fuqara. At the
beginning of my stay, I had been instructed to write
to the University, informing them that I had taken an
extended leave of absence, thus keeping the way open
for my return, should I wish to go. I had never expressed any desire to leave, each day taking me forward in its stride and showing me more wonders. I
had lost all sense of time. Yet when I was told that,
after the Moussem of the Master, I was to return to
the University and the life I had left behind, I felt
neither regret nor excitement. If that was where I had
to be, I was content to be there, but now that I knew,
somehow it made each day more precious to me.

The fuqara began to arrive for the Moussem of
the Prophet—wild, ragged men from the mountains
and lean, noble horsemen from the desert. Gently
spoken scholars with heads bowed and lips moving in
constant *dhikr* mingled with strange *majdhubs,* who
would spend hours singing passionately of the glories
of the Holy Prophet and his Lord. On the night of
the Moussem, word came down from Sayedina Shaykh
that the fuqara were to go to Wisal, the shanty town
that lay on the hills a few miles from Falah, and meet
in the mosque.

We clambered into whatever transport was available. Some of us were crammed into large old cars that scarcely seemed able to move with a normal load, let alone packed with people, while others set off in small delivery trucks and vans. Crushed together in the cold night air, the fuqara seemed unaware of discomfort, and the rocking vehicles burst with the invocations and praise of our Master's Diwan. We arrived at Wisal to be greeted at the door of the mosque by the Master's Muqaddim, a black man with a voice of great sweetness, who held his fuqara sternly yet lovingly in his sway with an authority that was unquestioned by them all.

The mosque was astonishing. How it remained standing was a miracle. If the houses of these poor people were broken-down, ramshackle affairs of corrugated iron, their mosque was almost a stabile of their architecture. It consisted of one wooden hut with several little improvised windows that let in both the light and the cold. The roof consisted of bits of sheet metal and wood, with large stones to stop it blowing away. On top of this, leaning at an amazing angle, was a rickety minaret of planks nailed together. It was purely decorative, for no one could possibly have gone into it, but it at least distinguished the shack from the other buildings in the settlement. The inside was bare—wooden floors covered with rushes and an arabesque of wood to mark the *mihrab*. In one corner, a straw mattress and some cushions had been prepared in honor of the guests. We said our two *rakaats* of welcome to the mosque, then sat around the walls in a growing circle, and began to sing the Diwan of Sayedina Shaykh. Mint tea was prepared on a charcoal brazier in the corner, and soon the assembly was alive with that concentrated energy with which these evenings always began.

The arrival of the Master was something that moved me more each time I was privileged to see it. The love that flowed between him and his murids was something that revealed itself richer at every meeting. He sat cross-legged in the corner, his white burnoose wrapped about him, his hands folded in front of him or touching finger-tips to fingertips, like the Holy Prophet. The murids moved forward without fuss and kissed his hand. He would greet them by name, always investing that mo-ment with a special quality of beauty and love that went directly to the disciple's heart. Soon the little mosque was filled with the folk of Wisal, and nowhere were poorer people to be found, and at the same time, richer. The gathering was suffused with love. It shone out of every face, and as the night wore on and the singing of the Diwan gave way to songs praising the Messenger, the gathering seemed so unified that it was almost as if one voice sang.

We were approaching the climax of the evening. Everyone stood while Sayedina Shaykh declared the litany of praise and glory and prayer upon the blessed Messenger and Slave of Allah. After each four lines, we joined in with our unified song of supplication asking the Lord's benediction upon the Prophet, and then, the Blessing over, we performed the Hadra. The imam moved into the center of the circle, and the sacred dance began. The spiritual energy was tremendous and vibrant with love. The fuqara swayed forward and back to the Divine Name, while a line of singers wove a filigree of chanted Qur'an that filled the heart with awe. The imam, as always, conducted the Hadra with great sobriety, but with depth and concentration, as he had been taught by the Master.

There was no doubt that, within a very short time, Lights had manifested inwardly to certain members of the fuqara, and the air was lit with the Divine Presence. It was at that crucial moment, when concentration should be purest, and when thought should cease and the worshipper become no more than the breath of the Name that issues from him, that I felt compelled to turn my head. There, just behind the row of singers, alone, cross-legged on the straw mattress, sat our Master. His eyes were shut, and his head moved almost imperceptibly to the rhythm of the Hadra. Light poured from him and filled the mosque. Everything moved, and he was still; everything vanished, and he remained. We were mere specks of dust in the burning radiance of his light. At that moment, I knew that he was directing the whole affair, that from some supreme state he gazed into our hearts and poured light where he was told from on high. Then, even as I felt the awesome splendor of his state, I grasped that he was nothing. If we were dust, he could not even be that, for what remained of him? He was consumed in divine power, but when the coal blazes, what is fuel and what is fire? A voice in my heart, in the very depths of my being, but a voice, said, *"Wa lam yakun lahu kufuwan Ahad"*—"And like unto Him is not anything." Thus, at the very moment that I glimpsed a fragment of our Shaykh's majesty, I was shown that he was naught and that there is only Allah. *Ahad. Samad.* One. Eternal.

Nothing could have prepared me for the arrival of the fuqara, for among their number were some who, in their profound spirituality and noble learning, will always remain incomparable among men. Their combination of humility, modesty, and dignity, coupled with knowledge and experience of the Unseen, presented me with a new measure of what a man was and could be. The perfection of our Master could be set apart as belonging to his unique station, but here was a gathering of men, who, each in his own station of gnosis, presented me with a lesson in what the nature of our being truly could become.

Of all their qualities, none was more immediately impressive and delightful than their courtesy to one another. In greeting each other, the man of superior knowledge always gave a fuller greeting than his companion, and this never failed to occur. If the man was ignorant, he could only turn the encounter into a piece of theater that robbed it of sincerity, obliging the wiser man to demonstrate the folly of extravagant welcome. Yet when the faqir was aware, he would always accept the double blessing of the more developed murid with sweetness and pleasure. One moved among men who, the greater their knowledge of this world and the next, revealed themselves as more and more unwilling to expound on any subject. The more exalted a murid, the humbler and more awed he became in the presence of our Master, the richer his inner life, the more impeccable his manners and his attention to the needs of others. If there was water to be taken around the gathering groups of disciples in the zawiyya mosque, it was the *saaliheen* who carried the jug and the glass. When water was poured to wash our hands before meals, they were the ones who carried the basin and the towel. It was enough to sit with these men, to eat with them, to walk with them, for one to be impregnated with the Sunna of the Prophet, and to pray with them was a treasure beyond price.

I recall one man's arrival at the zawiyya. We were gathered in a circle singing the Diwan, when he came into the mosque. I had begun to train myself to follow the habit of the developed murids as best I could and remain with eyes cast down, as befits a slave and a worshipper. In this way, one avoided distraction and benefitted nonetheless from the presence of these extraordinary men. No sooner did I practice this than it yielded a strange result. Very soon, I could sense without looking up when a man of great purity had arrived. On this occasion, I was suddenly aware of a radiant presence very near me and had to glance in its direction. He was in rags, his djellaba literally hanging in strips on his body, and he had a cast in his blue desert eyes, so that one beamed out to one side while the other shone straight ahead. From under his turban I could see tufts of reddish hair, and his heavy hands had the mottled, overwhite skin which sometimes goes with that coloring. Only a few teeth remained in his head, but his smile was dazzling and gave the impression that he was blind and at the same time incredibly happy. I could not resist later telling the imam of the remarkable sensation I had had of the man's spiritual power. Was I correct? I pointed out the stranger, who now sat with some other dervishes in another corner of the mosque. The imam smiled and nodded to me. "For some men . . ." (The imam's voice was hushed with awe as he spoke) "For some men, it is enough that Sayedina Shaykh give them a glass of water for them to attain *fana*—obliteration."

On the day before the Moussem, almost all the dervishes had arrived. There must have been about three hundred of them, yet everyone was fed from the small kitchen of the zawiyya and somehow everyone found a place to sleep. From dawn until well after the night prayer, the mosque rang with praise of Allah. Hadra was performed, and the Diwan constantly sung. There was neither fervor, excitement, nor tension, but rather a lightness, a sweetness, and a strength in the company that not one of us failed to experience.

All day long, lines of disciples waited in the *minzah* below Sayedina Shaykh's apartment until they were called to have audience with him. I went up to the salon, because I had heard that my friend the Muqaddim from the desert had arrived, and I was eager to greet him. When I entered, there were several very developed murids in the room. They had just come from the Master, and the air was tingling with energy. One man, gentle, head bowed, sat still in a corner. When I approached him, he raised his face, and it shone with light. Tears rolled unchecked down his cheeks, and all he could do was to repeat over and over, *"Tabarak'Allah, tabarak'Allah, tabarak'Allah."*

I moved away, as I had been taught, leaving him alone. In another corner was a small, elegantly robed man with a mane of wavy, electric-grey hair to his shoulders. His eyes were flashing, and as I approached him I picked up his vibrations. I was introduced to him, and he grasped my hand warmly. On contact, it was like touching a bare light switch. I felt the surge of power thrust up my arm to the shoulder, a direct current of energy passing from his body to mine. I wondered for a moment if I was hallucinating, but then I saw the imam laughing with the same happiness that lit the face of the man who greeted me.

"This gentleman is one of our power stations," said the imam, nodding at the unspoken question on my face. "You should spend some time with him."

The man began to talk, brilliantly, bubbling with laughter and making point after point with clarity and profundity. He continued to hold my hand, and as long as he held it I felt this strange flow into my arm. At certain moments as he spoke, his whole body would be convulsed and shaken by what seemed to be a massive electric shock that ran right up his spine, making his head jerk. Each time it happened, he would declare, "Allah!" and each time the others would lower their eyes and whisper a prayer, awed by the event.

"He is wondering what this is." The man seemed filled with laughter and seriousness in a way I had never before encountered. "This is the Lightning! The Divine Lightning! Read Qur'an. It will tell you. Everything you want to know is in Qur'an."

He laughed again, then let go my hand. He cupped his hands together, and we followed him in holding our hands together for *dhu'a*—supplication. He asked Allah's blessing upon me and the other murids who would come to the Master, upon the zawiyya, and upon our Shaykh and Master, the Guide to Allah.

On the morning of the Moussem, the singing and the Hadra began before dawn. Once more, the place rang with voices praising Allah, vibrated to the Divine Name in Hadra, and, at prayer time, echoed to the sound of the believers' heads on the rough matting of the mosque floor. Qur'an singers arrived from Nahb in the early afternoon. By sunset, the mosque was crammed with people. Against one wall, a row of divans had been arranged and cushions laid out. At the place where Sayedina Shaykh was to sit, a large woven rug had been fixed to the wall depicting the black cube of the Ka'aba* in Mecca.

At last, he arrived. The crush was incredible, yet he moved without difficulty to his place and sat as ever in stillness surveying the gathering, cross-legged, hands folded, lips sometimes moving in prayer. Every breath he breathed was the Divine Name, and from the moment that he entered the mosque, everything was changed. He was an unmoving pivot around which the whole feast wheeled. The singing continued, but it was deeper and more mysterious, with a sense of the Lord's majesty. Sayedina Shaykh sat there at the heart of all the activity, and each person in that mosque realized that he was

Ka'aba is the name of the ancient house of prayer built by Abraham to the One Lord on the site where Adam circled a hill in Eden. It is to this empty mosque in Mecca that all Muslims turn in prayer five times a day.

aware of them, uniquely aware. Occasionally, the Master would instruct that someone should be brought to him, and various disciples were led, dazed, to sit at his feet. The "powerhouse" that I had met in the *minzah* was seated on the right hand of the Master. All the time the singing continued, men would weave their way through the densely packed crowd, handing out glasses of mint tea and the dry sweet cakes that had been baked in the zawiyya and blessed by the Holy Shaykh.

I sat in the middle of it all and tried not to be swept along by the spectacle, and then tried not to try. I sang, head bowed and eyes shut. Again and again, some edge of miracle would move into my zone of consciousness, and I would look, all eyes and ears and sensory curiosity, as if I had learned nothing in my stay at the zawiyya. I watched a young imam from the mountains, as the tears flowed joyfully down his face and he mopped them with a spotless handkerchief. A minute later, he was sitting beside the Master, eyes shut, serene, singing the Diwan.

How can I begin to evoke the mood of radiant calm that suffused the gathering? The mosque was ablaze with Lights and illuminated by wisdom. I looked around me, and it seemed for a moment that this feast was not confined to a little mosque in a desert town, but that it extended across the planet, that it was no less than an acting out of that feast that is our life upon this earth. The Lord gives us to eat and to drink from our conception to the grave. Abu Yazid has said, "Your job is to feed me, Lord, and my job is to praise You."

I saw every sort of human creature at the feast. There were those whose sole concern was the tea and the little cakes and the friends they knew. There were those who were utterly distracted by the spectacle of the dervishes, the murids, and the Master. There were those who gathered into themselves something of the beauty of the occasion and the strength of the *saaliheen,* around whom could be felt the peace of the Unseen. Then there were the Pure Ones, drenched in the Lights of gnosis and knowledge, to whom this feast was but a shadow and an illusion, and who saw, beyond the mere play of images and perception, the glories of another world. And at the center, unmoving, the Pivot and Axis of the Universe, the Perfect Slave before his Lord, the Shaykh and Master of the Age.

I looked up and saw standing over me the guardian, Abd'Allah. He held a basket of cakes in his hand. He called to another helper and took from him a glass of tea, which he gave to me. He offered me yet another cake. I declined politely, and he smiled. "Eat. Drink. *Bismillah!"*

"*Bismillah!"*

I took it and sat with the tea in one hand and the cake in the other. I looked again at the guardian, and he was gazing into me as one shines a torch in the dark. After a second or two, he nodded. There welled up in me a love which bubbled and seethed as it surfaced like an artesian spring. I opened my mouth to say *"Al-hamdulillah!"*—"Praise belongs to Allah." No words came, but the desert soil was swirled away in cool, sweet water.

He leaned toward me and whispered into my ear. It was the first time he had ever spoken a whole sentence to me.

"You are now afloat on the deepest sea of Sufism. There is between you and the ocean . . . only this frail bark—yourself."

At the same moment, the voice of the Qur'an singer filled the crowded mosque.

"In the name of Allah, the Merciful, the Compassionate.

Did we not expand thy breast for thee
and lift from thee thy burden,
the burden that weighted down thy back?
Did we not exalt thy fame?

So truly with hardship comes ease,
truly with hardship comes ease.
So, when thou art empty, labor,
and let thy Lord be thy quest."

Two days later, I was to say farewell to the zawiyya and make the long journey back to my former life. I found to my astonishment that I was looking forward to taking up my life at the S.U. again.

The day following the Moussem was one of tremendous activity. Every moment spent with the fuqara was a revelation, and I sat in group after group absorbing what I could of their knowledge and their teaching. My last night was happily spent with a small group of the fuqara in the house of one of the Master's most beloved disciples. We sang late into the night, and the Hadra was brief, yet powerful and sober. It was only a few hours

before dawn that we went to bed. I rose for the dawn
prayer and then decided to snatch a few hours sleep after
the prayer and before the zawiyya awoke to its morning
activity.

I fell into a deep second sleep. Into my dream
came Sayedina Shaykh. He was standing before me
and he called me by name. He called my name again
and told me to get up and come to him. He wanted
to see me. I awoke abruptly and sat bolt upright. The
place was still and silent. It was a dream. What was I
to do? Supposing he did want to see me? Supposing I
had been sent for—and yet, if so, where was I to go?
I could scarcely force my way into his apartment at
this hour, and anyhow I had never entered his rooms
without instruction. Yet the dream was so vivid to me
that despite what muddled thoughts came, I rose hastily and donned my djellaba. I rushed out of the room
and up the stairs. Where should I go? I ceased to attempt to sort the matter out. I had to go to the Venerable Shaykh and I was determined to obey him. I
saw a staircase that I had never noticed before. I had
no idea where it led, but I went to it and began to
climb, hitching my djellaba as I raced up the steps two
at a time. I arrived at one landing and turned the next
corner. Just above me on the next floor stood my
Lord the Shaykh, waiting. I saw him and stopped
short. I hesitated between advancing to kiss his hand
in greeting and withdrawing as if I had intruded upon
him, but he stood there and waved me forward. I approached, knelt, and kissed his hand. He spoke my
name. He placed his hand upon my head. I heard him

call upon the Lord to bless me. Gently moving his hand again, he indicated that I should go back to my room.

When I returned to the room I could not of course sleep. I performed four *rakaats* and sat in the corner doing *dhikr.* The imam came in after a little. I had gone over and over the events of the morning, trying to recall their exact sequence, trying to measure precisely what had happened and how. Finally, I confided in the imam my strange story. He smiled and nodded.

"Yes. Yes. That's very good. Very good."

And so I took my farewell of the fuqara, my heart overflowing and yet full of joy. The chauffeur had been told to drive me to the station, and he waited patiently as I said my last goodbyes. At the door of the zawiyya stood Abd'Allah. He embraced me in a crushing grasp and prayed over my head. Then from the folds of his burnoose he pulled out a package wrapped in rough linen. He thrust it into my hand with a loud *"Bismillah."* I made to open the package, but he stopped me, his hand over mine. He pointed, as if to my destination. I understood. I said the greeting of peace, and he returned a triple blessing upon me, his face grave and gentle, and I got into the car beside the chauffeur. A moment later, the zawiyya was lost to sight. Half an hour later, I was on the train, and an hour after that, I was airborne.

On the plane I sat staring at the gift the guardian had placed in my hands. I longed to open it, but waited until I got home. Even there, something held me back. I called a cab and drove to the S.U.L., took the elevator, and walked along the corridor to my old office. The framed design was still on the wall, and once again I examined it carefully. The maze slowly uncoiled itself, and I saw that it was built up of Arabic letters arranged in a formal pattern. I read around the picture, and the Kufic script unfolded its message: *"Barakatu Muhammad"*—"Blessings upon Muhammad."

I sat down at Kasul's desk and placed the package before me. I started to undo the wrapping, and before I had finished I knew what it was he had given me. It was a book bound in dark leather and when I opened it I read on the title page: *The Book of Strangers.* It was in manuscript form and I recognized immediately the writing to be that of Kasul, the same hand that had written the notebook which so long ago had set me on my way. Abd'Allah! The book which he sought was his own. The knowledge he desired, he possessed.

The Hadith of the Prophet—on whom be blessings and peace!—came to me as I stared at the first page, unable to turn it: *"Man arafa nafsahu—fa-gad—arafa rabba-hu."* ("He who knows his Self—truly—he knows his Lord.")

I turned the page and read.

. . . After a long silence, Si Hamoud placed his hand on my arm and spoke: "There is a story told about the end of the world—how it would be. The vast numbers of the planet's population were sunk in ignorance and violence and frenzy. In one of the great mega-cities, throbbing with directionless, explosive activity, two withered, ancient women, forgotten, dying beggars, crouched in a corner watching the endless, terrible spectacle. One of the women turned to the other and said, 'It is awful. Look at them. Look at us all. I understand nothing. Why? Why this vast creation, this planet, these millions of people in misery? What is the meaning? Did anyone ever know?'

"After a long silence, the other woman placed her hand on her companion's arm and said, 'I remember, when I was a young girl, a long, long time ago, a strange man came to our city, begging. He was in rags like us and he wore a pointed cap. I can still remember the peace in his eyes as he put his hand on my arm and whispered to me, *La ilaha il'Allah.*' "

POST FACE

A Hadith of the Prophet Muhammad—on whom be blessings and peace!—records him as saying:

ISLAM BEGAN AS A STRANGE ELEMENT, AND WILL BECOME THUS AGAIN, AS IT WAS AT THE BEGINNING. BLESSED, THEREFORE, ARE THE STRANGERS.

He was asked who were the strangers, to which he replied:

THE STRANGERS ARE THOSE WHO RECTIFY WHAT PEOPLE HAVE CORRUPTED OF MY LAW, AS WELL AS THOSE WHO REVIVE WHAT THEY HAVE DE-STROYED OF IT.

(Al-Darimi, Riqaq, 42:
Al-Tirmidhi, Iman, 13:
Ibn Majah, Fitan, 15.)